NERDY LITTLE SECRET

CARRIE AARONS

I wrote this in the time of quarantine, six months pregnant, while watching my two-year-old.
This is for all the mothers.

Do you want your **FREE** Carrie Aarons eBook?

All you have to do is <u>**sign up for my newsletter**</u>, and you'll immediately receive your free book!

PROLOGUE
MICK

"You have to keep it down," I whisper in her ear, stopping the pump of my hips.

"Well, if *someone* would stop doing that swirl thing with his finger, maybe I could."

Jolie chuckles, but it's half-hearted and more a breathy moan than anything. Insider her, my cock pulses, impatient as a petulant child and wanting me to move again.

"I can't help it when you make that noise." I bury my nose in her mocha waves and inhale the scent of sunscreen and citrus vanilla body wash. "But if you don't stop, we're going to wake up every cabin in the vicinity. And then we'll really be in trouble."

Miranda, one of the head counselors at the summer camp we've both worked at for the last three months, has already caught us making out in the barn. *Twice*. I was so embarrassed; I was beside myself. Of course, Jolie just shrugged it off and said we could ask her to join next time. My jaw almost unhinged when she'd said that.

Never in a million years would I have believed you if you told me this is how I'd end the summer going into my junior year of college. I mean, I'd believe the part about working at a summer camp, because Camp Woodwin is one of the best-paying jobs a college kid could ask for. Sure, it's demanding work with twenty kids rotating through your cabin each week, and dealing with their fights, homesickness and so on, but it's not all bad. There are the endless hamburgers and hot dogs, which for me is great, the fun games and relays we run during the day. There's also a lake and an Olympic-size lap pool, so I get to not only swim myself but teach swim lessons. Plus, as I mentioned, I'm walking away from this summer with over two thousand bucks in my pocket. That's going to make a hell of a difference during the semester and allow me to not have to look for a part-time job and focus on my studies.

But the part about hooking up with the hottest girl I've ever encountered in my life? I'd have laughed in your face and asked which fan-fiction you'd been reading recently.

See, I'm a nerd. No, it's not a stereotype, I really am. In high school, I took every honors course available. I played the tuba in the marching band. My friends and I had weekly get-togethers to watch *The Big Bang Theory*, and we played Pokémon long after it was deemed not cool anymore. Medical textbooks and YouTube videos of surgical procedures interested me more than porn, and I wore a tie with the periodic table on it to my prom.

The only saving grace I have in terms of coolness factors is that I can swim and am damn good at it. I've won multiple regional competitions and hold the one-hundred-meter butterfly record at my high school. It's why I have some muscle tone to me, and the tan I've unconsciously worked on throughout the summer helps, I guess. Otherwise, I've still got the black-rimmed glasses and Star Wars T-shirts.

I have no problem with how I am, or where that puts me in terms of lunch tables or friend groups. I never have. I honestly really like myself and my life.

But this is all to say that a girl like Jolie Kenner would never go for me. Not in a million years. Not unless the stars aligned, we were stranded on an island together, or by some miraculous chance of fate, she decided she had nothing better to do.

Thankfully, for me, it was the third option.

We both started at Camp Woodwin the first week it opened in June, as one half of a pair of boy counselors and girl counselors in our respective cabins. The camp was co-ed, had twenty cabins in all, and housed a whopping forty-five camp counselors to watch after the rascals that were shipped in each week.

I met Jolie the third day in on the archery course since our cabins had recreation time together that day. My God, was she the most gorgeous creature I'd ever seen. Waves of chocolate hair down to the middle of her back, eyes to match that glowed like dark diamonds in the moonlight. On the day we met, she was wearing the tiniest jean shorts I'd ever seen, and her long, slim legs led up to an ass so perky, I had to keep sending my eyes skyward to avoid looking at it. Same with her chest, which looked far better than anyone else who was wearing the standard issue forest-green Camp Woodwin T-shirt that day. But it was more than just her looks; Jolie Kenner is the type of girl who effuses personality, sexiness, and something indescribable. She is the girl in every high school rom-com movie that walks down the halls and turns heads. You can't not look at her, and there is no way you can stop yourself from going up and talking to her.

Something I said that first day must have caught her attention, because from that point on we developed this flirty sort of banter that I ruminated on whenever I laid my head on my pillow. She'd tease me about my big brain, and I'd pretend to get her name wrong, calling her Julia. We sat at the same table for dinner each night, overlooking our campers but also having a fun battle of words ourselves.

And then, one night when we were loading the dock equipment and kayaks into the shed down by the lake, she kissed me. Backed me right up against a wall and kissed me.

Before Jolie, I'd only ever had sex with one other girl. Brenda McClure took my virginity our senior year of high school in a basement closet at a friend's house. She had braces and the frizziest hair that kept getting in my mouth, and I'm pretty sure it took me fifteen minutes just to put a condom on.

That demonstrates just how finessed and experienced I am when it comes to members of the opposite sex. Sheesh, I had to write a snail mail letter to one of my buddies to make him send me a package of condoms since I couldn't leave the camp. I never even kept a stash in my wallet, that's how much I *wasn't* anticipating getting laid as a twenty-something male.

From that first kiss, things only escalated. For the last two months, we've been sneaking out at night, rendezvousing during our breaks, and hooking up any time we can be semi-alone. We're like addicts, two of those lovebug flies that attach together and can't seem to separate. I've taken more risks trying to have sex with Jolie than I've ever taken in my life. Danger is the furthest thing associated with my name, but this summer, I've let myself look it straight in the face.

Not only has she taught me so much about what women want, but Jolie has taught me not to be so serious. To take life in moments as it comes, no matter the consequences.

"Oh, *Mick* ..." She groans, as I bend her over the counter in the canteen.

It's a favorite meeting spot of ours, because it's always dark after eleven p.m., and we can sneak a candy bar from the stash in the back after we're done.

Her ass slaps against my groin as I pound into her, my hands flexing at her hips. All of that chocolate hair is laying over the counter, and she's looking up at me, almost daring me to make her be noisier.

God, this girl.

My hand slides past her hip, down to where we're joined. Flattening my finger, I press the tip against her throbbing bud, swirling it around in circles just the way I know sets her off. As I jut my hips and try to hold off my own climax, I press harder, rub faster, and try not to think about how this will be the final time.

I feel Jolie tense up, her body giving all of its telltale signs of orgasm. And when she lets out a careening wail, I cover her mouth, absorbing the sound in my palm.

I'm not far behind, seeing stars as my knees buckle and I spill into the condom.

When I fold in half, covering her body while we stand, still connected, I plant kisses on her cheek. A second later, she taps my arm, silently radioing me that she's uncomfortable and wants me to get off. I pull out, already missing the feeling of her.

"What now?" I ask, breathless, as I zip my khaki shorts up.

Jolie slips her camp-issued khaki skirt back into place, and I bite my tongue in disappointment. Never again would I see her beautiful body, hear her chuckle in my ear as my hands roamed in places they'd never be again, or talk with her until the wee hours of the morning. This had become more than a hookup to me, which both surprised and saddened me. I never thought Jolie would be the kind of girl who I'd be able to have a connection with aside from the physical, but she's really become a friend. We talk about fears, feelings, and have a real humor between us.

"We go back to real life. We call this the perfect summer and put a bow on it." She shrugs, as if none of this affects her.

I have to shut off the part of me that cares, the one that wants to ask to keep in touch or figure out how to continue this. Because she's right, though she doesn't know why she is on my behalf. This was my last hoorah, the perfect end to a summer that was about living carefree and taking risks. I'm not this guy, but I allowed myself a short break to pack some fun in before my life turns serious and studious.

In the fall, I'm off to a new university, one that will propel me, hopefully, into medical school and the career I want beyond. I have no time for distractions, for sex or love or anything that I know Jolie would provide.

So, I pack those feelings away. I've been prepared to do that for six years now, dedicate my life to a cause greater than me. Jolie, or any relationship with a woman, would just be one more thing I'd have to give up.

"It's been nice coming with you." I extend my hand for a shake.

Her palm meets it, and the tinkle of her laughter is the soundtrack I'll play in my ears for months to come.

1

Someone curses down the hall, and I wake to the smell of burning hair and last night's tequila.

"Ugh," I mumble, my mouth tasting like ash and bad decisions.

Pulling myself from bed, I inspect the mess and assess the damage. Well, I managed to get myself into some semblance of pajamas, even if that means I'm wearing a T-shirt from my eighth grade soccer team and the bodycon skirt I wore to the bar last night. On my bedside table is a glass of water and a half-empty bottle of Advil, which explains why, bless the universe, I have no headache this morning. My room is its usual clutter of discarded outfit ideas, disregarded textbooks, and too-sophisticated decor for the dump of a college house I live in. I told my mother as much, but she insisted on shipping in some comforter from Paris and a desk chair from Sweden, so here we are.

"Maddy, did you burn yourself again?" my roommate Christine yells down the hall from somewhere else in our house.

"This fucking curling wand gets way too hot, and now it looks like there's a hickey on my forehead," Madison, our third roommate, whines into the dark hallway.

My feet feel like sludge as I trample over high heels and silk blouses to get to my doorway. "Put some Neosporin on it, it should go away within the hour."

"Ah, look who's joined the land of the living. Didn't think we'd see you until noon." Christine whizzes by me, smelling like lavender and toting a breakfast pastry.

I almost try to take a bite out of it before she scoots around me. "What the hell happened last night?"

"Too much tequila and a last-minute decision to go to the hookah bar," Maddy yells from our one bathroom.

Which explains the taste of ash in my mouth. My stomach whines as I head for the kitchen.

The three of us met freshman year and were instant best friends. Madison is the music major, destined for concert halls and fame. She plays the harp, and it's so beautiful, it'll make you cry. She's also the nicest of our bunch, always reaching out to make plans or get us into the best parties or places. Then there is Christine, the shrewd businesswoman. I swear, she'll be biting her male employees heads off like a praying mantis one day. She's the smartest one, the friend who uses common sense and makes sure we pay our cable bill on time or don't get evicted.

Then there is me, the glue that holds us together. I wouldn't say I'm smart or talented, unless it comes to kissing or clothes. If you need help in the beauty department, I'm your girl, which is why I'm majoring in business with a branding minor. If I could get into a beauty company, make my own products or market theirs, that'd be the best fit. If I have to work, I might as well do something I like.

I'm also the wild one, the friend who forces us to take risks so that our memories during this time don't just shine, they sparkle.

But of us, I'm the most reckless, the most irresponsible. Which is why my best friends are already up and at 'em for the first day of junior year courses, and I'm still working off a hangover.

Our kitchen is surprisingly clean, which I'll attribute to Christine. She's always drunk tidying, which works well for me. If I lived in our three-bedroom ranch alone, I'd have burned the house down ages ago while trying to make nachos at two a.m.

"Don't steal any of my Frosted Flakes!" Madison scolds me, still in the bathroom.

I put the box back, cursing her in my brain, and take down some of my Special K strawberry cereal instead. It's just not as sugary, and I need some massive comfort food to power through this bad decision.

"What time are your classes?" I ask, trying to gauge how creative I have to get with my day.

"I have a nine a.m., eleven a.m., and a two p.m., so I'll be on campus most of the day," Christine answers from her room at the back of the house.

"And I have almost the same plus heading to the gym after. Anyone want to come to Pilates with me?" she asks hopefully.

Christine and I both make non-committal grunts, which is how our conversations about exercise usually play out. Maddy asks, and we rebuff.

"How about you?" Christine asks, referring to my class schedule.

I've thought about this all summer, how much I'd have to hide or sneak from them. I thought it'd be easy, but now that it's here, I'm not quite sure how I'm going to do this. They'll be all over campus all day, and while we swim in a sea of ten thousand students, there are still likelihoods they'll ask me where I was all day.

Our ranch sits on a street about two minutes from the Salem Walsh University campus in North Carolina. It's a road lined with college houses, each one fixed up just enough by its owner to be trashed and then recycled to the next college party kids next year.

I'd picked Salem way before I ever graduated high school. Basically, before I'd even gotten to the seventh grade, for several reasons. One, it's my parents' alma matter. Two, the university was one of the best in the state, not to mention country. And three, it's twenty-five minutes from the beach.

Salem Walsh University has all the crawling ivy on its buildings and a sun-drenched quad to look like one of those picturesque colleges in a movie, but with a beach town feel. After class most days, students head for the shores to surf, study on the sand, or play a little volleyball before the bars open for the night.

Except this semester, I wasn't technically one of those students.

How am I going to hide this from my best friends? From everyone? What if they ask which buildings my classes are in this semester, or want to meet up for lunch?

I got myself in a world of trouble, being as reckless as I am. But I've done half my time. This summer at camp was the first part of my sentencing. Now I just have to get through this year, and senior year would be golden.

I just have to figure out how to avoid telling my roommates, and everyone else I know, that I'm going to community college.

2

MICK

Turning in a wide circle, I feel like a kid on Christmas who just opened the full Encyclopedia Britannica.

This campus is far better than the pictures, and if the outside is anything to go off of, I'm going to love it here. Lush grass, red brick buildings, lampposts with every graduating class year stamped into them dating back to nineteen fifteen. Dorm buildings with the school's mascot, a Jaguar, hang in the window, and students dotting every spot on the quad with colorful textbooks, laptops, and blankets.

And that's just the landscape. I've pored over the course catalog for Salem Walsh University for months, and when it came time to schedule, I loaded my lineup with the hardest credits offered.

Most of the kids here probably wouldn't have done the same, overloading their course schedule with more credits than actually allowed, but I got special permission. Not only am I a transfer student, but I'm trying to graduate by next fall, with a summer semester added in. With extenuating home circumstances and the path I want to take in my career, administrators at Salem Walsh agreed to let me do what I wanted.

See, it was embarrassing and awkward to tell people where I was going to college during my senior year of high school. With my grade point average and SAT scores, I could have gotten into an Ivy League school. Unfortunately, when you're the son of a handicapped father and a mother working three jobs to pay the bills, it's just not in the cards.

So, I did my first two years at a community college five minutes from my house, to have the ability to take care of my dad while mom worked and put a roof over our heads. He was diagnosed with ALS six years ago, after function in his hands started to decrease. The diagnosis was a shock to all of us, after all, my dad was the kind of a person who ran marathons. He was healthy, fit. He wasn't the type of person who got a life-altering disease.

Six years later, he's bound to a wheelchair and slurs his speech so badly, that most of the time he doesn't talk at all. It was essential I was home for those two years, to feed him, change him, give him his meds, and basically be a full-time care-giver. Finally, after three years of waiting and applying and pleading with the right people, my father was approved for full-time home care.

Which means I get to attend a real college. Going into my community college, I had already qualified out of most of the required courses due to my AP credits. That gave me a leg up, allowed me to take sophomore level courses as a freshman, and I just continued down that path. Now, as a first semester student at Salem, I could take my senior classes as a junior, take courses through the summer, and graduate in September.

And hopefully, be enrolled in medical school by December. I had a plan, one that had formed the day my Dad was diagnosed, and I wasn't going to slow down for anything.

Walking through campus, I spot the building I'm looking for. Monmouth Hall, my dorm.

It's three flights up and six doors down before I'm knocking on the place I'll call home for the next nine months.

"It's open!" someone calls, and then I hear a bunch of mumbling.

Tentatively, I open up the door, and to my surprise I'm not hit with the stench of weed. Exhaling in relief, I push it open more to reveal what looks like a common room. There is a guy sitting in a gaming chair, completely ignoring me in favor of his headset, screaming at someone on the screen. Looking at the game, I see he's playing *Call of Duty*, and I gingerly set my bags on the floor.

"Hey, I'm Mick Barrett, your new roommate?" It's more of a question than I intend it to be, but whatever.

The guy, lanky with a brunette chin strap and shaved head, flicks his glance up to me, and then furiously hits his controller, bullets spraying on the television.

Another person walks out of what looks to be a small kitchenette.

"Yo, who's this?" a short, stocky guy wearing a Kiss Me, I'm Irish T-shirt asks the guy in the gaming chair.

I extend my hand. "Mick Barrett, your new roommate."

"Your name is Mick Barrett? That doesn't fit at all." He shakes his head and doesn't take my hand.

I've heard this a lot throughout my life, and I don't disagree.

"My dad is a huge rock fan, and since our last name is Barrett, it couldn't work better. Syd Barrett from Pink Floyd? He's like one of his heroes. And then he was a big fan of Mick Fleetwood and Mick Jagger, so he convinced my mom to let them name me Mick. Little did they both know, they'd be getting the most un-rock-like nerdy son in the history of the world."

The guy on the floor pauses his game. "Sweet, I love Pink Floyd. I'm Martin, that's Rodney, and Paul is off sleeping somewhere. Or maybe he's at the library, I can't remember."

I nod. "Nice to meet you guys. Didn't realize this was a suite."

"Yeah, we all have our own bedroom, though the twin beds suck ass. We have a rotating chore schedule, someone to clean the bathroom or kitchen every week 'cause I'm not a dirty-ass person. Hope that's okay," Martin says.

"Good with me, I'd rather things be clean." I thank my lucky stars at this moment that I got some decent roommates.

Well, who knows if they're decent, but at least they won't leave beard trimmings in the bathroom sink or curdled milk in the fridge. Anything else, I could probably live with.

"You guys are sophomores?" I ask, knowing that I'm one of the oldest people probably still living in the dorms.

Rodney nods. "Yeah, we're looking to get our own off-campus house next year, but this dude's mom wouldn't let us this year."

He punches Martin in the arm, and his friend scowls. "Whatever, it means we still get meals in the dining hall."

"You're a junior? A transfer, right? I think I lost the piece of paper they gave us on you." Rodney shrugs.

I nod. "Yeah, a junior, but trying to graduate early. Mind showing me which is my room so I can unpack?"

For two guys I hardly know, they seem pretty nice. They like video games, which I can hang with, and witty T-shirt sayings, so I think we'll get along fine. They show me to my room, which is at the back of the suite. It's small, no more than a twin bed, a desk, and a dresser, but it will do. It's the first freedom I've been afforded away from my parents in nearly twenty-one years, so it's more than adequate.

After I unpack most of my clothes into the drawers and make my bed, my stomach is rumbling.

Walking out into the living room, I meet Paul, my third roommate, and ask about food.

"Anywhere I can go to get a good sandwich?"

"We can take you to the Pub. It costs money, but it's much better than the dining hall. You should get one good meal before the crap in the cafeteria." Martin picks up his room keys.

I follow, kind of excited to be traveling with a group of semi-friends around my new college.

3

JOLIE

My bag keeps swinging and hitting me sharply in the hip as I jog into the Pub, Salem's on campus pay-per-meal dining area.

I guess that's what I get for being reckless. Every action has a reaction, or a consequence in this case, and mine is having to tote around a massive bag of textbooks while I sneak from one campus to another. It's been three days of classes, and I'm still not adjusted to my new way of being a student.

The Pub is cooler than the dining hall, and it's got better food too, so Christine, Maddy, and I typically meet in here for lunch. It got its name because back in the day, you used to be able to buy alcohol here before the campus became dry. Now it's just a large lounge/study/eating space where students occupy tables for hours at a time, and a salad costs ten bucks.

When I finally get inside, relishing the cool air-conditioning as it smacks me in the face, I'm met with hundreds of students talking and eating. The place is mobbed, as is expected, but it doesn't take me long to find the spot of our usual table. The walls are done in our school's navy and gold colors; the booths are smooth leather, and the floors gleam a dark hardwood.

Madison and Christine sit in the massive ten-person booth that we've claimed as our own, surrounded by our athlete friends and some of the girls they date. There is Charlie, the quarterback of the football team, Darell, the pitcher for the baseball team, Andy, who is the school's leading wide receiver, and two more of their friends. Beside them sit Britta and Eileen, Charlie and Darell's girlfriends, respectively.

"Jolie!" Britta waves her hands, her olive skin glowing even more with its summer tan.

I smile, waving as I walk over. "Good to be back, huh guys?"

I managed to sneak away from the campus that none of them know I'm attending to bust my ass over here for lunch. I have to be back in an hour and a half, and that's calculating the twenty-minute drive it takes me to get there.

"So good. Life is boring without college. I'll even take the classes." Charlie puts one beefy arm around Britta.

"He says that now." Andy snorts, chucking a fry at his quarterback's head.

Madison makes a choking noise. "Ew, you almost got ketchup on me."

"Glad to see we still retained our table." I set my bag down, fishing around for my wallet. "I need to get a salad."

"Oh, the cash part of the machine is broken, so they're only taking Salem cards, just FYI," Christine tells me.

My heart panics, beating against my chest. "Um, could I borrow yours? I actually left mine at home. You know I'm good for it."

She hands her ID card over without another thought, thank God. I don't know how I would have thrown out another excuse on the spot. I can't damn well tell them the real reason, that my ID card was deactivated due to me not being a student here this year.

After I wait in line and grab my strawberry balsamic salad, I head back to our table.

"We were talking about hitting the pool later, you in?" Eileen asks, and I have to avert my eyes from Darell practically biting her throat like a vampire.

Those two were separated by three states all summer, so it looks like they haven't wasted any time now that they're back.

"Sure," I say between forkfuls. "We doing chicken contests again?"

"Are we fifteen? Why are we still doing that?" Christine rolls her eyes.

I point my fork at her, talking to the group. "She's just mad that I completely owned her last time. Andy, partners?"

The wide receiver looks me up and down. "Of course."

We had a brief fling freshman year that fizzled out when he hooked up with a sorority girl and I saw his tongue down her throat. Since then, we've remained friends, with him trying to get in my pants every shot he can. I've said no each and every time. I love hookups, love sex, but once you betray me, or I have to smell another girl on your sheets, I'm done.

We lapse into a conversation about classes; the guys start hypothesizing wins based on teams they're playing this year, and Eileen keeps bringing the talks back to a hilarious new Netflix show she's watching.

Out of the corner of my eye, a familiar head of swooping auburn locks catches my attention. And in an instant, I can't believe what I'm seeing.

"Mick?" I cry out, completely unaware of where I am.

He halts, looking around at the sound of his name. Clover-green eyes land on me, and those full lips quirk up in his signature smirk.

"What the heck ..." He looks as genuinely shocked as I feel.

Before I think about what I'm doing, I jump up and into his

arms. Mick hugs me back, albeit awkwardly, since we're in a cafeteria full of people. I guess when you hook up in the shadows all summer, it might feel weird to express attraction out in the open.

"What are you doing here?" I smack his chest, which is clad in a shirt that reads *B is for Beets*, with a picture of that weird guy from *The Office* on it.

Mick points at himself, his green eyes sparking with shock and amusement. "I go to school here."

My mind feels blown. How had we not talked about this all summer? "Have you always gone here?"

"No, I just transferred this year. How did I not know you went here?" He seems to be having the same thoughts, though his eyes are wandering down my legs.

A sizzle of attraction burns through my spine, and I'm aware of how much sexual tension there still is between us.

"Guess we never talked about." I shrug, a smug grin painting my lips.

We were too busy fucking each other's brains out and sneaking around the summer camp we both worked at.

It surprised me, how drawn I was to Mick Barrett. His name sounds like that of a rock star's, but the guy couldn't be further from the moniker. Even now, his surprisingly hot physique is trapped in the wardrobe of a nerdy teen. A graphic tee, jeans that don't fit his ass right, sneakers more scuffed than a country line dancing floor, and those glasses.

Scratch that, the black-rimmed glasses are pretty sexy. Mick is pretty sexy, though not conventionally. He's a strawberry-blond, so almost a redhead, which makes girls overlook him. But those green eyes are blazing and his bone structure is that of a lean cowboy or something ... I'm just drawing from the smut novels I've read. He's a swimmer, so his body is perfection, but he hides it all under the unassuming clothes and quiet personality.

Mick is Prince Charming wrapped in tinfoil, and he's the best damn lay I've ever had.

That's when it comes back to me, the reality of where we are. Three guys stand next to Mick, and they all look young or too skinny. Maybe I just hang out with the beefcakes at my table all day, and so I notice their structure more. They're all gaping at us, and the short stocky one is clearly staring at my boobs.

"Um, Jolie?" I hear Maddy from behind me and turn to see our entire table looking at me.

Nine pairs of eyes blink at me, curious, weirded out, and my two best friends look at me like I'm an alien. Here I am, hanging onto a strange guy in the Pub, and he's not my typical type.

I take two steps back and slick a hand nervously through my brown waves. "Uh, yeah, this is Mick. We ... worked together over the summer."

That's when I notice I can't even make eye contact with Mick. What would my friends say if I told them about what had happened between us this summer? Christine and Maddy didn't even know I'd been mandated to work at the camp by the court as my community service. How would I explain Mick and why we know each other?

"You worked this summer?" Andy chuckles in disbelief.

"I didn't realize Daddy wasn't paying for the country club membership this June." Darell winks at me, teasing.

"Yeah, it was nothing really. Good to see you, Mick. Hope you enjoy Salem."

And with that, I climb back into my booth, not making eye contact with Mick again. Inside, I'm burning with shame. What the fuck is wrong with me? Am I a high schooler, trying to prove my worth to the table of popular kids?

Yes. That's exactly what I am, as horrible as that is. I just have too much to lose, too much that can be uncovered and harm me even worse than a summer fling I still seemingly have feelings for.

I only allow myself to glance up once, and the look of disappointment is not the one I expect to see on Mick's face.

Disbelief, maybe, disgust, sure. But disappointment? That cuts deeper than anything.

Mick Barrett sees right through my bullshit, and it's almost as if he expected this kind of rejection from a girl like me.

As shitty as I felt about myself this morning with everything I have to carry, and all that I have to make up for, this makes me feel the worst.

I'm the exact stereotype people have always pegged me as, and it never hurt quite as much than when the one boy who I could have really felt something for looks me in the eyes like that.

4

JOLIE

Four-inch wedge sandals were the wrong choice today.

It could also be the fire-engine red fit and flare dress I have on too, or the pearl clips I put in my hair. I keep forgetting that Salem Community College is a very different place than Salem Walsh University.

I've gotten no less than sixteen strange or leering looks as I've walked through the tiny, rundown campus carrying my designer bag full of textbooks. Two catcalls, some scathing stares from girls in the tiniest jean shorts with their belly button rings sticking out under crop tops. I look like some kind of pageant girl in a land of trailer parks.

Okay, that's mean. I know that. Salem CC isn't very different from my high school, with all sorts of types of people who belong to all different types of social classes. I'm just bitter about being here and choosing to put on the opposite of rose-colored glasses when it comes to this place.

It's been exactly eight days of me being an enrolled student here, and not only am I still struggling with classes at the lowest level of college possible, but I'm so uncomfortable here I can barely drag myself to campus. The whole landscape is gray, aside from the patches of dirt in the untended lawn. The buildings, the windows, the doors—all shades of doldrum and it's honestly depressing.

There are no students flocking the measly quad, or clubs and sports teams advertising their latest game or membership opportunity. The professors in my courses are monotone and seem overworked. A lot of the kids don't even seem to want to be here.

As I walk into my biology class, the hardest of my course load, at least three people roll their eyes.

"Don't worry, they're just jealous because they can't afford that Chanel bag," a voice comes from my right.

Looking down at the desk next to where I'm standing, I see a girl with wild curls dyed the color of a lavender bush. Her skin is porcelain white, and her eyes glow this interesting color of amber. She's striking, and I'm not sure why I haven't recognized her before. She's also wearing black jeans and a black tank top on a blistering ninety-degree day, which makes her even more interesting.

"You recognized this as Chanel?" I point to my bag, hefting it onto the floor and sliding into the desk next to her.

Violet-haired girl shrugs. "I like material things."

That makes me chuckle. "Me too. I'm Jolie."

"As in Angelina?" She smirks.

I shrug. "My mom had a thing for the movie *Girl, Interrupted* when she was pregnant with me."

"So are you named after the psych ward patient, or the actress?" She still hasn't told me her name.

"Both, I guess. Depends on which day you catch me on," I joke.

The girl seems to weigh this, and then her amber eyes catch mine. "I'm Jennifer."

Jennifer seems too plain a name for her, but I don't tell her that. "You a junior?"

"Yep. Stuck in this suck-ass place since I have nothing better to do. I should have transferred out to a four-year school last year, but my parents can't afford it. So here I am, getting another associate's in some major I'll never perform work in. But it sucks less than working at the mall round the clock, and that's the deal if I want to stay under their roof. School or a job."

Her openness about her predicament hurts my heart, but she surprisingly doesn't seem to mind it.

"What's your story, Girl Interrupted?" She rounds on me, interest flickering on her face.

No way am I divulging what I did to get me stuck in here. "I'm a junior, and like you said, basically I'm just a girl whose life has been interrupted."

It's my own fault, too, but we're not going to get into that.

"Are you bombing this class, too?" she asks, flipping through the secondhand textbooks we were handed on the first day.

"Yeah, it's so difficult. What's with this guy? It's like he doesn't want us to pass his class in a ... malicious way."

Both of our heads turn to the front of the room as our professor, a man who had to be in his sixties that insisted we call him Dennis, is setting his old leather briefcase on the desk. We had moved so quickly through cells that I nearly had whiplash and were now onto DNA. I could barely understand what he was talking about, much less study the book work we were supposed to do every week.

"Good morning, ladies and soldiers." Dennis gives us his usual greeting, which I find bizarre. "Who studied their genetic profile from Wednesday?"

He'd given us a discounted membership to 23 and Me, and we were supposed to see our genetic makeup.

It didn't really matter for me; it didn't tell me anything I didn't know. I'm part Persian, part Italian, just like my mother and father always told me. But how wild would it be if you discovered you were supposed to be one hundred percent Israeli and you were actually Danish or something? Talk about adoption suspicions ...

A bunch of students raise their hands, and Dennis launches into the biology of DNA.

Fully aware that I'm supposed to be soaking in as much information as I can, instead, I tune out. I can't help it. This classroom is too warm, since the community college has the shittiest air-conditioning I've ever come across. Plus, I plan to have a full on study session with myself, and I'll lock myself in the library if I have to this weekend.

Also, I have something else on my mind.

I've been thinking about sending Mick a text since I saw him in the Pub almost a week ago. I feel horrible for the way I treated him, how I basically shunned him. I hadn't even bothered introducing him to my friends, or trying to ascertain how he'd come to be a student at Salem. It was a bitchy move, and I was a coward.

The world I came from was all about status. The way you looked, how much money you had, the pretty things you wore or cars you drove. Being the most popular, having the hottest boyfriend, those were things that were praised in my hometown and even my household. When you grow up in that mindset, in any mindset really, it's hard to break out of it.

That's a horrible thing to say, that all I've been molded to focus on are appearances and wealth, but it's true. Since I've been in college, my mind has been opened in ways I didn't anticipate, but I still go home to the world that made me. Conditioning is a real bitch.

Then I met Mick, and he flipped my world upside down. He

was everything I'd been told to avoid, and yet, he was the most hypnotizing guy I'd ever been around.

If I'm being honest with myself, I want him again. So without overthinking it, I pull up a text, type his name in, and hit send.

Jolie: *Hey, hope you're having a good time at Salem so far.*

There. That's not overly desperate or inquiring. Maybe I should have apologized or asked him to grab lunch—

No, shut up. Stop second guessing yourself. I've never doubted myself over a guy, not even with my biggest crush in high school. He was a senior when I was a freshman, and I'd been the one to invite myself to his prom. I was overly confident when it came to men, a fact I could be proud of, and was also a huge flaw.

It made it extremely difficult to get close to someone, to let down my scary guard enough to show them the girl underneath all the pomp and circumstance.

I get no typing bubbles, no read receipt, not anything. Even at the end of biology class, which lasts well over an hour, Mick still hasn't returned my text.

Nor does he almost three days later, though I keep it in my inbox, the unanswered message taunting me.

This is the most rejection I've ever felt, and the feeling pricks at my chest like a hundred thorns. Well, fine, whatever. If Mick Barrett doesn't want to talk to me, then I don't want to talk to him.

As if that's not the most immature response on earth.

"Elections for student council are happening now, people, sign up!"

"Love to dance? Come audition for the Salem Walsh University Dance Team!"

"Rush Alpha Omega!"

Apparently, I didn't get the memo that today was clubs and activities sign up day. As I walk through the main thoroughfare of campus, shouting voices and peppy pledges shout at me from every direction. Everyone wants you to sign up for their club, from Jews for Jesus to The Magic Club.

No really, there is legitimately a kid in a blue and gold cape pulling doves out of his hat in the middle of the quad. Which kind of intrigues me, but not enough to join in and see that train wreck every week.

I have enough to occupy my time, what with taking the hardest courses that have ever been thrown at me. Quantitative Techniques for Biological Systems, Human Anatomy, Molecular Control of Metabolism and Metabolic Disease, Topics in Cell and Regenerative Biology Stem Cell Seminar ... and those are just my Monday, Wednesday, and Friday classes.

That isn't to say I don't love it. The information is challenging, the ways of learning are innovative and so much more advanced than that of the community college I was attending. My professors are renowned in the science world, and I can feel my knowledge growing with every passing minute.

I've been a student at Salem Walsh for nearly two weeks, and I've done little else but go to class, complete papers, and study. I was happy to do it. Remember, I'm a nerd. I take pleasure in doing school work, when my peers would rather go out and drink themselves into stupors.

My phone vibrates in my pocket, and I pick it up as I sit on a bench in the quad, aware I only have fifteen minutes before my next course.

"Hey." I smile as the FaceTime call connects, showing my parents sitting in our living room back home.

"Bud!" Mom exclaims, probably more excited that she got the video call to work rather than me being on the other end of the screen.

"How are you guys doing?" I ask, knowing Dad is not going to say hi.

He does this little kind of wave thing, and although I should focus on the happiness of talking to my parents, all I can do is assess his current physical state.

"We're good, for the most part. I cooked a chuck roast for dinner, so we'll enjoy that. Those mockingbirds are back at the feeder in the backyard. Dad is watching that documentary on vegetarianism you recommended."

Mom talks for both of them, and I smile. Even though my father is sick, she still tells me about the mundane aspects of their life. That's my mom, the positivity squad. She's had a hard go of it these last few years, but you'd never guess it from her attitude.

It's the first time, aside from working at camp this summer, that I've been away from my parents for an extended period of time. We were a unit, us three, and it felt weird not being with them. I'd been a big part of my father's everyday care and attempted rehabilitation, so to not be there gives me an enormous sense of guilt and anxiety.

It also sounds corny, but they were my closest friends. Although I had two or three friends, I would hang out with in high school, I was a homebody. I read, or built model ships, played video games ... you name the dorky thing and I did it.

"How ... sc ... school?" Dad asks, slurring out some words.

I don't miss a beat. "School is good. My classes are really challenging, which is great. I have a clinical during the second half of this year where we're going to be doing tests with lab rats. Nothing that harms them, but just testing different foods, exercise methods. I'm excited."

Hands-on work was bound to be my favorite. I will revel the day I get to put on scrubs and a white coat and start hospital rotations.

"Oh! We also had a doctor's appointment two days ago. With that specialist who is doing the clinical trial," Mom mentions, like it just slipped her mind.

I smack my head, because I even forgot that they did that. I should have called two days ago to find out what happened and feel guilt burn a hole through my stomach.

"How did it go?" Anxiety flows through me.

Mom shrugs. "It was okay. They did all of the regular tests his neurologist usually does. But in the end, they said he unfortunately isn't a candidate for the trial."

That burns. I'd been calling that office for months, trying to get Dad in for an appointment to be considered for the trial. That's what I did in my spare time, called hospitals and doctors and every program imaginable to try to find a cure for my father.

"Why won't they consider him a viable candidate?" I ask, anger infused in my tone.

"I'm not sure, they just said no." My mom's voice sounds indecisive.

Annoyance ripples through my veins. "But you didn't press them further? This really could have helped, Mom."

Shock flashes through her eyes. "I know that, *son*. I'm doing the best I can. If they say he's not a candidate, then we'll try to find something else."

"Shtahpp." Dad tries his best to put up a curled hand, his fingers no longer able to extend themselves in a flex. "No ... fighting ..."

Just those words took effort. We can both see it. His eyebrows don't move into an angry scowl at my mother and I sending barbs back and forth, and he's drooling a little from the corner of his mouth.

This disease is stealing every part of him, and it's heart-breaking to watch. I wish I could slow time down, for his sake, but speed it up. If I could get through school at a quicker pace, become the kind of doctor I'm dreaming of being, and then discover a cure ...

It's a pipe dream. One I know people have been working on for way longer than I've been thinking about it or since my father has been diagnosed with ALS. But it still doesn't make me want it any less.

"All right, well, I have to go to class. I'll talk to you guys later, okay?"

Mom sighs. "Okay. Love you."

"Love you, too," I say, and press the button to end the video call.

Emotion clings to my throat, disappointment and frustration ripe on my mind.

After we hang up, the call flashes on my phone and ends,

taking me back to the screen I was previously on. It's my text message screen, and they're all laid out before me. Not that there are many, I barely talk to anyone on a daily basis. I had it open, about to text Martin to ask if the guys wanted me to bring them some beer back for their Friday night hangout, since they couldn't buy it themselves.

Typically, I wouldn't have bought for underage kids. But they were just shy of twenty-one and only drank two beers each on Friday nights while they played video games. It was harmless, and I was grateful for pretty easy-going roommates.

My eyes stray to the unanswered text from a number I thought would never contact me again. Jolie's name taunts me at the top of the text, the one I didn't reply to.

Man, did I want to. Truly, I did. But then I remembered her look of ... detachment in the Pub. The way her friends snapped her back to reality, and suddenly I wasn't her Mick anymore.

I was the nerdy guy she shared a few secret hook ups with at summer camp, the place no one even knew she'd gone. Or so I suspected. The look on her face, like she was trying to hide me and everything else from those people in that big booth ... it took me right back to every rejection I'd had.

It's not like I'm not used to women friend zoning me or not seeing me as an option to date or kiss. I get it, I give off a certain vibe. I'm not the jock walking around like the world can see his penis. I'm not the sexy musician who will play the guitar naked in your bed. I'm not the bad boy who will leave you at a party but then call you the next night and profess his love. Girls want that kind of thing, and they're lying most of the time if they say they just want a nice guy.

I am the nice guy, and believe me, no one is banging down my door.

The fact that Jolie had texted me that vague sentence that you'd send to an acquaintance was offending, too. She could have at least apologized, or said she'd blanked and hadn't introduced me to her friends. Maybe she could have asked to see me, since it was a weird freaking coincidence that I'd ended up transferring to the same college she studied at.

When she yelled my name in that dining hall, time stood still. Swear on my life, I never thought I'd see Jolie Kenner again. I'd made my peace with it, dreamed about her almost every night since we left Camp Woodwin, and pushed past the urge to text or call her. And then, there she was. As usual, she looked like something sent from heaven. My God, I knew how beautiful she was, but not seeing her in a month or so only magnified her attractiveness.

As Jolie threw her arms around me, all I wanted to do was take her back to my dorm room. Undress her, talk to her, catch up on the things that had happened since we'd been apart.

But her expression of near horror confirmed everything. I don't need that drama of chasing a girl who believes she's out of my league. I don't need to lust after someone who is clearly more concerned with her social status than the actual character of the guy she's sleeping with. There are far more important matters to attend to, namely the thing I'd just had to bite my tongue about on the call with my Mom and Dad.

After shooting off the beer text to my roommates, I lock my phone and throw it back in my pocket.

Time to do the thing I came here for; focus on my studies and graduate as soon as possible.

6

JOLIE

If you'd told me a year ago that I'd be spending a Saturday afternoon in the library, I'd have fallen over clutching my stomach in laughter.

As it is, before this year, I hadn't stepped foot in the place. My freshman and sophomore year classes, while challenging, weren't that big of a deal. Most of them were fashion merchandising, or I could pass with a C in courses like math or science. But now, it's As or bust, as mandated by the disciplinary board that reviewed my case.

So, library on a weekend it is, and it has to be the Salem Walsh one. They have better textbooks, Wi-Fi, and I honestly feel strange going to the community college one.

Plus, Salem's is just so pretty. With its red brick and floors of quiet nooks and the musty smell of old books, it just encourages one who hates studying to *want* to study. I've also Elle Woods-ed myself; If you dress in an outfit that makes you feel like a businesswoman, with the glasses to match, and a fierce high pony, then you'll retain that much more information. Or at least that's what I'm telling myself.

I'm just about to waltz through the machines that prevent students from stealing books from the library, when the clerk calls out.

"I need to check you in."

Fuck. I did not see that coming. I didn't even realize you had to check in to the library, but I guess it makes sense.

My heart is racing as I walk over, and the guy asks to swipe my ID. Shit. I send up a Hail Mary prayer, hoping for the best.

"Sorry, your ID isn't working." The kid sitting behind the desk hands it back to me. "You'll have to go get it fixed before I can let you in."

I stutter, trying to come up with an excuse. If I ask him to run it again, it'll be like one of those bad dreams where they cancel your credit card at some highly expensive restaurant and everyone is staring at you.

I need to study, and I know that if I don't get to in here, I really won't do it. My grades, my future, depend on this one library session, as it's all I can control right now.

So, I lean into the desk, making sure to push my boobs together. Immediately, his eyes are drawn down, and I flutter my lashes as I start talking.

"Ugh, it's just so annoying. This thing has been on the fritz for weeks, and every time I get it fixed, the swipe strip deactivates again. I *reallyyy* have to study for this biology exam I have. Could you maybe ... swipe it again?"

His eyes flick back up to mine, and his tongue is lolling halfway out of his mouth. He scans the library, trying to see who might be looking at us, and then swivels in his chair to look behind him.

"All right, go on in. Just don't tell anyone, okay? By the way, are you—"

I jet off before he can get his question out, which I know will definitely have something to do with my relationship status or openness to hookups.

"Now I see how you get yourself through life," a voice mumbles just as I'm about to dump my books on a table near the banks of computers on the first floor, and I spin to see who it is.

Mick is walking past me as he plucks something off the reference desk, not bothering to turn around and say much else. That note of disappointment, the same one I saw in his expression the other day, is clear in his tone.

"What?" I cock my head to the side, because this is a strange greeting.

And if I'm not mistaken, he's clearly judging me.

"Nothing." He shakes his head, chuckling to himself, and then attempts to walk away.

"Really? Hi to you, too." I raise an eyebrow, annoyed.

"Hi, Jolie. Have a nice study session." And with that, he walks off, planting himself at a table piled high with books, on the other side of the first floor.

I glare at him, hoping that my attitude pierces his ridiculously large brain, because how dare he. He was definitely just making a comment about how I flirted with the clerk to get in, and I'm pissed. Yes, I did flirt to get in, but Mick is making a judgment about how I live my life.

With my temper flaring, I march across the library, studying be damned.

"What are you trying to insinuate?" I practically stamp my foot as I stop in front of his table, crossing my arms over my chest like a child about to throw a temper tantrum.

Mick sighs, saving something on his laptop, and then sweeping those rainforest-colored eyes up. "Nothing. I didn't mean anything. Just forget it. Truly, I hope you get your work done. Now, I have some I need to get done."

But the annoyance doesn't simmer down in my chest. "Why are you being so weird?"

I actually sound like a five-year-old, but I can't help it. I've never cared what anyone thought of me, though I know some of the things they call me. Spoiled, rich girl, bratty, entitled. That's fine. If they don't want to get to know the person I am on the inside, I've never really minded.

But something about Mick, a guy who knows me more than maybe anyone ever has for the short period of time we've spent together, judging me ignites my blood.

Maybe it's the fact that he's never acted this cold toward me. This summer, we not only formed an intimate attraction, but we had a friendship. Mick was always there for some fun banter or to listen to me vent about my bitchy campers. He was never once cold or dismissive, not like he'd just been a minute ago.

He just smirks. "I'm being weird? Come on, Jolie, let's not get into this. We had a good summer, and we both go to school here now. We don't have to do this awkward, let's-be-friends or let's-figure-things-out deal. You made your feelings known in the Pub the other day, I'm okay with that."

God, I hate that he's the most honest, level-headed person I've ever met. The dramatic part of me wants so badly to make him blow up, to trigger something that sets him off. But everything I'm trying isn't working.

"You're seriously mad about that?" I try putting words in his mouth.

Someone down the row of tables shushes us, and Mick shoots me a dirty look. Oh, my bad, I'm getting him in trouble in *his* kingdom.

Mick is still seated, which is pissing me off further. I'm used to guys tripping over themselves for me, and the one that I want attention from can barely rise to his feet to have a conversation with me.

"Jolie, what do you want? You balked the other day when your friends saw what I looked like, though I have a feeling they don't even know who I am to you. And after basically dismissing me from your table, you decided to text me like I was your partner from study group who came down with the flu who needed well wishes. As if we don't even know each other. I'm just following your lead, so if you don't want anything to do with me, I'll be happy to sit on another floor of the library and do my work."

Gah, he's maddening! I loathe his rationality at this moment.

"Why didn't you answer my text?" I ask, having nothing to lose.

He runs a hand through his auburn hair, and I'm annoyed at how much I want that to be my hand. "Did you really want me to? We agreed to end this. Plus, what was I supposed to say to that?"

I shrug, not wanting to admit that he's right and I'm wrong.

"Why doesn't your ID work?" Mick asks, and I know his obnoxious intelligence is trying to sniff me out.

I'm asking him annoying questions, so now he's going to try to push my buttons.

"You heard what I told the kid at the desk, the strip keeps deactivating."

Mick looks skeptical. "Yeah, how many times has it done that?"

"Four." I make up a number on the spot.

"Why wouldn't they just give you a new ID card?" He knows that we both know I'm lying.

Mick sniffing around in my business has all of my walls flying up. It was a stupid mistake coming over, trying to instigate him. It was never going to work. And now he's just trying to get under my skin, discover what I'm hiding.

Without another word, I turn on my heel, taking my secrets with me. He's right, after all.

We don't have to talk about all of this. The less I talk to anyone I don't absolutely have to, the lower the risk of having to spill all of the bad behavior that led me to this point.

Plus, I have enough studying to shut me up for a year.

T wo hours of studying later, and I'm ready to pack it in.

It is a Saturday night, and I think I've earned a little fun, even if it's just a small gathering at Paul's friend's house. I'll go for a drink or two, and then it'll be back to my dorm room. Tomorrow, I have a full docket of programs and trials I want to try to get Dad into, and a bunch of emails to write to internship programs.

I'm eyeing one with Dr. Francis Richards, the foremost expert on Amyotrophic lateral sclerosis, or ALS. He runs one of the most high-tech, innovative laboratories in the country, and it just so happens to operate out of the Salem Walsh University Hospital.

There was a reason I picked Salem as the college I wanted to transfer to. Aside from its stellar biology program, it has one of the best medical schools on the East Coast. And Dr. Richards is just the cherry on top. I know I'm only a junior, and it's difficult for even third-year medical students to get onto his rotation, or shadow him period, but it's worth a shot. I'm hoping that if I can convince him to look at some of the research I've been working on, on the side, he'll be interested enough to let me intern for him even if that means simply fetching his coffee.

I pack up my last book, relinquishing my table, though there is barely anyone else here on a Saturday night.

Even though I try my hardest not to, my eyes float to the other side of the library. There sits Jolie, gnawing on the end of a pen cap in frustration. Her hair is tossed this way and that, there are crumpled sheets of paper littering the floor under her feet, and she looks nearly on the verge of tears.

Damn, maybe I was too harsh before.

I couldn't help it, when she came over, trying to start something with me. She was the one who had all but shunned me in the Pub days ago, and now she had a bone to pick because of some offhanded comment and my view of her was twisting into something uglier than before.

Before I got to Salem, I had never viewed her in the way others had at camp. There were whisperings that her father owned the place, or she was there as some kind of penance. I never asked because it wasn't my business. Others thought she was snooty and privileged, but I got to know the real Jolie. The hilarious, intelligent, vulnerable side of her. She wasn't the bratty, spoiled rich girl everyone assumed she was. I'd seen her get down in the mud during tug-of-war, stack supplies in the lakeside dock rooms, and get up every day before dawn with one of her campers who had an especially bad time of the month.

She has a heart, one I don't think she lets a lot of people see. And for that reason, I wander over to her table to apologize.

"Tough study session, huh?" I peer down at her, trying to ignore the familiar scent of her hair wafting up at me.

That citrusy vanilla, like she's been bathing in orange-flavored cupcakes. The smell used to cling to my clothing long after I'd returned to my own cabin, and it's intoxicating now.

"As if you'd know what that's like." Her tone is pouty, and she doesn't look up.

"Actually, this Metabolic Disease course I'm taking is giving me a run for my money." I chuckle, trying to make light of my own intelligence.

It doesn't work, and Jolie still stares down at her paper, scribbling notes in the margin.

"Listen, Jolie, I was—" I'm about to say harsh when she interrupts me.

"Why the hell do I need to take biology to work in makeup anyway?" She practically breaks her pencil in two with how hard she throws it down at the table.

There is no one to shush us now, with everyone all but gone and getting ready for their wild Saturday nights. Without her permission, I pull out the chair across from her and take a seat.

"Well, I guess it would have to do with the product makeup. The different elements of the makeup, what it does to human skin or lips, that sort of thing, right?"

Jolie finally looks at me, those inky brown eyes rolling in my direction. "I wasn't looking for an actual answer, Boy Genius. It's fucking stupid is what it is. I know how to get women to wear makeup, I know *good* makeup. That should be enough. This study guide doesn't even make sense, it could be in Mandarin and I would be able to read it more clearly."

"Let me see that." I pull her study guide from her hands and look to see what she's completed thus far.

And that's when I see it. The Salem Community College logo stamped at the top of her work packet.

"No, give that back." Panic is written all over Jolie's face as she tries to snatch it back.

"Where did you get this?" I ask, holding it on the other side of my body where she can't get it.

There is a beat that passes, one of her looking at me with so much panic and emotion in her eyes. I see it all so clearly now. The way she didn't introduce me to her friends. The "broken" ID and flirting her way into the library. Her near hysteria over a study guide.

I know this feeling all too well, because having been a student at community college, when you could be attending a university deemed way more publicly acceptable, brings a certain level of shame. Even if there shouldn't be one.

"You're not ... you go to a community college?" I whisper, as if someone might hear us.

"No." Jolie cuts me with her eyes, her mouth an angry slash to match.

I level with her, giving her an earnest look and handing the study guide back. My silence causes her to break.

She lowers her head, moving her face closer to mine. "Fine. Yes. But if you tell anyone, I'll cut your goddamn balls off."

I almost bring my hands down to my crotch, because the threat makes me wince. I know Jolie isn't joking at this moment.

"Why would I tell anyone? And who would I even tell? I was your friend, or so I thought. I wouldn't do that." The thought that I'd even consider it in her mind kind of hurts.

A flash of guilt passes through Jolie's eyes, but then it's gone. "It's not something I'm broadcasting, and I'd appreciate it being kept a secret. And no, I don't *go* to community college. I'm just ... temporarily a student there."

"I'm not sure those things aren't the same thing." I tilt my head to the side.

She lets out an annoyed huff, like I'm making her spill the beans even though she's being purposefully evasive.

"I ... got into some trouble. And was *given the option* to rejoin the Salem Walsh student community during my senior year if I complete and receive As during my junior year at a community college."

Tapping my chin, I consider something. "And the time as a camp counselor this summer? That was punishment, too?"

"Punishment is a harsh word." She waves her hand as if I'm putting too much of a spin on something that is clearly a punishment.

"You were given community service?" I guess, trying to make her tell me the whole story.

I don't like dishonesty, and right now it's starting to piss me off. I'm a straight-forward, rational guy. Always have been. I don't like drama and I don't like lies. Jolie seems to come chock full of both of those, and it's temporary insanity that must be keeping me sitting at this table.

"No, I never went to court." More swerving my questions.

"What did you do?" I fire back.

Jolie looks away, fidgeting with her hands. "I don't want to talk about it. Didn't you need to study on your own, anyway?"

"I'm done. Anyways, guess I'll leave you to it." I shrug, not feeling the urge to do what I came over here for.

Why should I apologize now, if she's being this evasive? I don't put up with any of these personality traits for any other person, so why should I for Jolie? She's been nothing but callous and unnerving since I discovered we both go to Salem Walsh—well, at least one of us does. I'm not going to give her a pass just because we have a history and she's the most gorgeous girl I've ever laid eyes on.

I begin to walk away until I hear her small voice.

"I'm probably going to fail."

The sadness and despair in that one sentence has me turning around. Because even though it's against everything I've just convinced myself of, Jolie Kenner is apparently my kryptonite.

She's wallowing in her study guide, and I swear she might just cry. So I utter the words that I swore I wouldn't from the minute she showed me that biology study guide.

"I'm a biology major. I could tutor you."

8

To this day, that night is blur.

Well, not all of it.

When I sat in the dean's office in nothing more than an oversize Salem Walsh University T-shirt with dripping wet hair—that part was completely sobering.

I'm not sure who thought we should do the dare, or who proposed it. At some point during one of the most epic fraternity parties I'd ever been to, someone had suggested we go alter the statues in the iconic fountain on campus. Naked.

Of course, I was six tequila shots in and thought this was the funniest idea ever proposed on earth. Plus, I'm known to shed clothes when the drinks come out, so a romp in the cool fountain on a hot fall night sounded like the best thing ever.

I don't even know how many of us took the hike to campus, stripped down, and climbed into the fountain. There are four statues installed in the large fountain, which is more like an Olympic lap pool than the kind of fountain you see in someone's backyard. They are of the Greek gods for music, science, and two more that I forget. And they all have anatomy that is *very* visible.

So it was only natural for drunk, moronic college kids to

bring cans of spray paint, *naked*, into the fountains, as we sprayed their boobs, cocks, and vaginas with all the colors of the rainbow. In the moment, it was the most hilarious thing I'd ever done. We were cackling our heads off, and the others must have run off when they heard the sound of the sirens.

But stupid me, I was either too drunk or too wrapped up in my art project to hear them. Until campus police were shining their headlights on my bare, wet ass.

Which is why I ended up in the dean's office, at midnight on a Saturday, with no underwear or bra and my eyeliner running down my face. In all my life, I'd never been in so much trouble.

As far as my friends were concerned, my father had handled it all. There was nothing, according to them, that Mitchell Kenner couldn't handle. Especially if it was a measly thing like tampering and nudity on a college campus. He'd fixed tabloid scandals, gotten murderers off charges, made millions for companies who definitely didn't need it and had escaped apologizing to the middle-class workers they'd fucked over.

My father was the highest-paid lawyer on the eastern seaboard, and normally, he'd always fixed every problem in my life. If I needed a wheel greased with a teacher, or a better part in the school play. The time I had a bad time slot for school pictures, or when my friends and I got caught in tenth grade smoking pot at a local park. He fixed it all. I was his baby girl, his only child, and he wouldn't let any shit stick to me.

But this ... this he could not fix. People saw the spray paint the next morning, and rumors began to fly. Professors were offended, and donors were furious. They had to blame someone, even if the dean announced that a student had been accordingly punished in a private manner and didn't announce a name.

So it fell to me. Of course, I was no snitch, I would never rat anyone else out. Though they tried, they tried like hell. The dean—who was friends with my dad—and my own father tried to bully a list of names out of me. They didn't want me to go down for this. But I was already there, campus police had already found me and no one else. No sense in getting someone else in trouble.

My grades were also less than stellar, a fact the dean kept highlighting. Both of them agreed that I could use a little tough love, that I was taking things for granted, and so, I would have to pay for that. My father was the one who offered up the idea of a summer job, any cause that was close to the dean's heart.

His brother-in-law is the one who owns Camp Woodwin, and so I would work there for three months as a camp counselor. For *free*. Fine, that didn't seem so bad. I could get through the bugs and lack of reasonable outlets for hair tools.

But the dean wasn't happy enough with that. So he proposed a year of academic probation, and a stint at the community college. If I passed with flying colors, I'd be admitted back into Salem Walsh for my senior year, with no mention of the punishment on my permanent record at the college. My degree would come from Salem Walsh, and no one would be the wiser.

It was a fucking awful compromise, but I was backed into a corner. And now, it was a bitch keeping the secret.

Well, not from everyone. I don't even know how Mick figured it out so quickly, except for the fact that he had some kind of enormous genius brain. The minute he knew, I was so embarrassed I could die. It was bad enough that he was like, the smartest guy I'd ever been in the presence of, but now he knew I couldn't even keep my grades up enough to attend the college we were both supposed to go to.

He kept pressing me for information, which only made me feel like more of a loser. If he knew what I'd done to land myself in this position, he would think so much less of me. Shit, I don't know how his opinion of me could get any lower, with how I'd treated him and now with what he'd found out about me.

Him offering to tutor me? I never saw that one coming. Mick was just too caring and too honest of a guy, and I felt like an asshole taking advantage of that. But ... he could teach me more than I could ever learn on my own. He was a freaking biology major, for crying out loud. I couldn't not take him up on it.

And I wanted to see him again. That electrical charge that had always sparked between us was still there. I thought about him, about the sex we'd had, *all* the time. When it's that good, you can't not crave it. And man, was I craving it.

"Are you ready to go?" Maddy pops her head into my room.

I slick one last coat of matte lip-gloss on my mouth, and look in the mirror, primping. "Yeah, I think so. I can't believe it's already the annual jungle party."

Her tiny two-piece cheetah outfit highlighted her long, lean body. "I know. I feel like we just got here and now we're on the cusp of one of the best parties of the year."

The football house, the one where Charlie and Darell live, always throws an epic jungle-themed party in the middle of September. Christine, Madison, and I had all gone shopping for our outfits last weekend, pulling together scraps of material that covered our most essential bits. I had on a white leopard two-piece that was nothing more than a bathing suit top and mini-skirt.

"I have fireball shots ready on the counter!" Christine yells from the kitchen.

Madison races out of my room, and I comb my fingers through the curls I twirled into them tonight. Since the two of them think I got off scot-free from the fountain incident, they think it's business as usual. I'm always down to drink, no matter what night of the week it is, and by drink I mean party my ass off.

I'm the ecstatic kind of drunk who only gets happier as the night goes on. Dance parties, pranks, sappy conversations, that's me. I've been gifted the ability to drink copious amounts of alcohol without getting sick, and it's just *fun*.

But now, after everything that's happened, I'm more cautious. Each weekend we've gone out, I stay lucid enough to probably drive, which isn't my normal. I have to pretend that I'm as drunk as my friends, and I'm on edge a lot.

I can't risk getting myself into more trouble, at least not this year. But that doesn't mean I'm going to miss out on my favorite moments with my friends.

So I take the Fireball shot with my friends and then resign myself to water and lime the rest of the night.

It seems like I'm keeping all kinds of things hidden these days.

9

MICK

"No, he needs to be doing more of the hand bike exercises. Yes ... yes, I understand that, Bernie, but he was really making good progress with that before I left."

Dad's physical therapist argues with me on the other end of the phone, saying something like if I think that, then maybe I should come home and exercise with my father.

I have to bite my tongue so hard, I swear I taste blood.

"Of course, I'd like to do that, Bernie. Unfortunately, I'm at college, working to get a degree so that I can help my dad even more than you are!"

This conversation has gone on for five minutes too long, and I really shouldn't snap at him like this. He's done a great job with Dad so far, and I'm just getting on his case for not accepting my input. He's the expert, but I'm the one who knows Dad best. It's rude and ungrateful to yell at the people who are helping to care for my father, but I'm at my wit's end.

And him suggesting that I'm not around enough for my family is like pouring acid in a gunshot wound.

Bernie says something in a clipped tone and tells me not to

call him anymore. That if I have a suggestion, I can send it through my mother. And then he hangs up on me.

It takes everything in my body not to throw my phone at the brick wall of the room I reserved in the library. I'm just so fed up. Nothing with Dad's treatments has gone right this week. His neurologist saw decreased hand motion at his appointment on Thursday. The gastroenterologist claims that he may need a feeding tube soon if the muscles in his throat don't allow him to swallow enough food. And now I've got Bernie on my case, because he should be doing everything in his power to *increase* Dad's mobility, not decrease it.

And on top of all that, I have my first study session with Jolie today. We agreed, after she texted me again asking for a date and time, that we'd meet on Friday at two in the library. I reserved us a room, since I didn't need any more dirty looks thrown my way if she decided to pick a bone with me.

But my nerves are up to my ears and my temper isn't far behind it. I'm usually a pretty level-headed guy, but the stress of being away from home has intensified since I've been at Salem Walsh. I've been focusing so much on my own studies, securing an internship, and forming some kind of friendship with my roommates, that everything else seems to be slipping through the cracks.

Add Jolie on top of that, and I'm one eye twitch away from being committed.

Looking at my watch, I see that Jolie is already five minutes late, and that ticks me off even more.

Another minute goes by, and then the door to the room bangs open, a swirl of burnt orange dress, a gauzy olive scarf and her signature scent swirling around in a tornado of hecticness.

"Sorry, sorry! I really didn't mean to be late, but I stopped to get us coffees." She sets the two to-go cups from the Pub down on the table.

I do a bit of a double take, surprised at the thoughtful gesture. Part of me was expecting her to show up late, but not because she was grabbing me a coffee.

My eyes are also glued to her. Every time I see Jolie Kenner, it's like being blinded by car lights on the other side of the road at night. You know they're coming, but they still temporarily blind you, leaving spots on your vision long after they're gone. Jolie's beauty is kind of like that. It whacks you like a beam of light right to your cornea, and you can't focus on much else until she's long gone.

Jolie pushes the one she must have gotten for me toward my side of the table. "Black with two Stevias, right? I thought I remembered correctly."

And now I'm even more floored. I didn't even think she remembered me two seconds after she got in her car to leave Camp Woodwin, and here she is remembering how I take my coffee? The panic and ire that had been causing my blood pressure to double suddenly starts to dissipate.

"Yeah, thanks." I sip on it, observing her as she unloads her bag onto the table and then pops into the seat across from me.

"So, we're working on chemical bonds and intermolecular forces, which is basically gibberish to me. Ask which foundation works best on oily skin, and I'm your girl. But this? I don't compute."

Jolie laughs self-deprecatingly at herself, and I can't help but watch the way her mouth forms a smile, or wonder if she still tastes the same in that spot right beneath her earlobe. Her dark eyes assess me, and there it is. That zing of electricity, of recognition, that's always been between us. Suddenly, I gravely regret the decision to get a private room. We're alone in here, on the fourth floor of the library, and I haven't heard or seen anyone in the twenty minutes I've been sitting in here. There isn't enough space between us, the walls feel like they're forcing us in, like they want to make us talk.

I clear my throat, grappling for normalcy. "Actually, the exact science of what foundation works best on oily skin can be attributed to chemical bonds and intermolecular forces. So let's try to frame it in that way."

Jolie nods slowly, but I know she isn't nodding at what I just said. She's acknowledging it, the heat bubbling up between us. I don't have any room for that in my life, so I put my head down, ignoring it. Does part of me want to push all the books off the table in a frantic moment and take her right here? Yes.

But the rational part of me, the one who just got off the phone after arguing with a professional physical therapist, knows there is no sense in that.

For the next half hour, we put our heads down and focus on the work. This is secondhand to me, I completed most of this biology work in high school. Reading these studies, working on science problems and hypotheses is to me what makeup and fashion is to Jolie. I speak the language fluently, and I never really had to learn it.

I know for her, though, that this is like trying to learn Italian as a thirty-year-old. It just doesn't stick as well as it would for a toddler. So I reframe the study guide, put it in terms that she'll understand. After some initial hiccups, we start to get on the same page. I've never tutored before, but I've been in plenty of study groups, so I know how to work with someone else over shared scientific knowledge.

We complete almost half of the study guide before the hour I've designated to tutor her is up, and before I know it, we're packing up.

Something like nostalgia or homesickness clings to the air, and I can't help but look up at Jolie when my books are safely in my backpack.

Her brown eyes are hooded by those impossibly black, full lashes, and there is a slight flush to her cheeks. She looks innocent at this moment, when most of the time Jolie looks fierce and intimidating.

"So, do you need help next week?" I ask, hesitant.

I really shouldn't be offering, but I can't help myself. It felt good to accomplish something, to help someone. I couldn't do anything to further my dad's treatment, but I could do this.

"Yeah, that would be great." She nods. "I ... I really do hope you're liking it here. Salem Walsh is a great school, and I know you're so smart."

Neither of us has made a move for the door. "Thanks. Yeah, I'm really enjoying it so far."

A beat of silence passes.

"How much do I ... um, owe you?" Jolie fidgets with the strap of her purse on her shoulder.

She could have taken an axe to my heart and it would have hurt less. Christ, is this how it works in her reality? She pays the hired help so she doesn't have to feel guilty for hiding the fact that she slept with them previously? Am I just her charity case?

"I'm not doing this for money. Is that what you think? Jesus, you really don't think highly of those not in your financial stratosphere."

Brushing past her, I narrowly miss hitting her with my shoulder. It's aggressive, and I'm pissed off.

I hear Jolie's sandals clacking behind me as I make for the stairs. "Wait, Mick, that's not what I meant ..."

Beyond furious, I whirl around. "You're a real piece of work, Jolie. I offer to help you because it's kind and the right thing to do, even after you snubbed me. I did it because it seems like you're in deep, and forgive me for being so goddamn naive, but I thought we actually shared something this summer! You really are everything I always warned myself about. Keep your money. Good luck getting back into Salem Walsh."

Bursting through the staircase door, I take them down two at a time, hoping like hell Jolie isn't following me. When I get to the bottom of the library, winded and spitting mad, she's nowhere to be seen.

Figures. A girl like her would wait for the elevator to do the work for her.

O ur ranch house bumps with the vibrations of a Spice Girls song as Madison's epic pre-game playlist echoes through the house.

"Tell me what you want, what you really, really want!" Christine sings as she floats through my door.

She looks incredible in a skin-hugging black dress and high-heeled sandals.

It's still warm even though we're teetering on the edge of October, and we're going to take full advantage of the weather before we all have to cover up in sweaters and jeans.

"If you were a Spice Girl, which would you be?" Maddy asks as she comes in, flopping down on my bed.

"I'd be Sporty," Christine talks over both of us.

Maddy and I share a look and then crack up. "No, you wouldn't."

"What? She's serious and determined, like I am." She puffs out her barely covered breasts.

I shrug. "Sure, but you're also bossy, can be cold, and you have the little black dress to boot."

She pouts her lip. "Fine, it's a tie. Who are you two, so I can shoot those theories down?"

The flat iron runs over my hair for a last pass through, and I listen as Madison goes.

"Baby Spice, for sure."

I nod in the mirror, looking at them as they sit on my bed together. "Definitely. Sweet, a little naive, and totally cute."

"And you?" they both ask in unison.

"Duh, Scary Spice." I give them a devilish smirk.

They crack up, nodding in agreement. "You're the one who is always daring someone to go further. I also don't think you've ever been scared of anything."

Christine's words hit that nauseous, sick feeling in my gut. If only they knew how scared I am right now.

I failed this week's quiz in biology, and I feel like drowning my sorrows. After Mick blew up at me in the library, I texted him a few times to apologize. And after a few days had passed, I even swallowed my ego and asked for his tutoring help again. Because surely, without his expert way of reframing the subject for me, I am going to fail the class.

He'd never answered, which apparently was how he was going to handle all of my communications from now on. I feel like a grade-A bitch. The way he took it is absolutely not what I meant by it, but looking back, I can see how stupid of me that was. Of course, Mick was just helping me because he was a nice guy. But I was used to people only doing stuff for me or wanting to be close to me because of my money. Because of who my family is. It wasn't until I got to Salem Walsh that I saw how true friends operate, and it's hard to break that mindset.

Now, I'd not only screwed over the one connection I had to possibly scoring a passing grade and becoming a full-time Salem Walsh student again, but I'd completely severed my relationship with Mick. I'm not dumb, I know that there was a moment in that library room that we almost tackled each other across the table. Anything I was wishing could still happen between us has been extinguished, because of my asinine, loose lips.

Lord, I think I need that drink right about now.

So I know what I said about cooling down on the partying, but I've earned this night of reckless fun. As long as I keep it to drinking and remaining in my clothes, I'll be fine.

"Okay, how do I look?" I ask, twirling around to show them my outfit.

I picked my shortest, high-waisted black shorts, the ones that practically mold to my body. I've paired them with a bright white crop top, that has a dotted, lace shell over it. And the black, six-inch scrappy sandals I'm wearing only add to the outfit.

"Killer." Madison smirks.

"Like you're on a mission to do something *bad*," Christine agrees.

"Perfect, that was just what I had in mind. What are we drinking?"

We venture into our kitchen, where liquor bottles in all stages of emptiness litter the biggest counter. We all stand in front of it, surveying the options, and Madison pulls down our colorful array of shot glass options from the cabinet above. The glasses have been collected over our two, almost three, years here. There are several with different locations we've vacationed at, one with the Eiffel Tower from my trip to Paris last winter. One simply has a penis in the middle of it that lights up neon colors when a switch is flipped. There is another that reads "Oh, just swallow it, you've had bigger things in your mouth than this."

They're all either raunchy, sentimental, or hilarious, and we love choosing one each night. Tonight, I opt for a dark pink shot glass that has the ingredients for a cosmopolitan on it, and then grab a bottle of raspberry vodka.

"That raspberry vodka literally gives me flashback dry heaves." Madison looks like she might be sick, and we haven't even taken a shot yet.

Christine cringes. "That's what the 99 Bananas vodka does to me. Remember, I almost had to have my stomach pumped?"

I nod, remembering that awful night. We all have one, the liquor that makes us dry heave even if we're in the middle of a class on a Tuesday afternoon or watching a movie over break with our parents.

I raise my hand. "Gin. Gets me every time."

My friends pick their glasses and poison of choice, and we all dole out a shot.

"To being Spice Girls," Madison proposes, and then it's bottoms up.

As we take the first shot, it burns my throat.

And tastes like one epic night on the way down.

11

MICK

There is absolutely no reason I should be in a place like this.

It's louder than anywhere I've ever been before, and I'm pretty sure the seventh circle of hell isn't this hot. The whole place smells like grain alcohol and sweat, and I'm pretty sure I have both of them clinging to my skin, put there by other people. I just saw a girl vomit into her Solo cup, and I'm pretty sure there is a couple on the makeshift dance floor in the living room actively having sex.

I sip my beer, leaning against the wall at the first college party I've ever been to.

Actually, this is probably the first party I've *ever* been to. As I said, I wasn't big into them in high school, and going to community college and caring for my sick father didn't really lend itself to getting drunk underage in the last two years.

When Martin insisted we go to this party, I was ninety-five percent against it. Really, I was going to stay in and study. Maybe watch a few episodes of *Curb Your Enthusiasm,* maybe order myself a burrito from the local Mexican takeout place.

But then they'd tossed a beer in my face, Martin all but

bullied me to come check out this girl he'd been hooking up with, and Paul claimed he needed advice on how to get a girl from his statistics course to give him the time of day. As if I had any relationship advice of value.

Really, I think they wanted a designated driver to the party off campus, but it felt kind of cool to be included.

Though, I was thoroughly uncomfortable. The guys outlawed any of my outfit picks, which included a Battlestar Galactica T-shirt, and another long sleeve that depicted the best scene in *Jurassic Park*. Instead, they made me wear my darkest jeans, which were tighter than the pairs I'd normally opt for. And then Rodney loaned me a dark maroon T-shirt that clings to my chest and biceps. I look like every other guy in here, and it's kind of strange.

But at the same time, I've felt the eyes of some of the girls following me from room to room. It's a welcome surprise. Not that I have time for that, of course.

"There she is, there she is." Martin taps me rapidly on the arm, and I settle my pretty much full beer in the other.

I'll be their responsible one tonight, since I am really not into this party. My eyes swing to the way he's pointing, and there is a curly-haired blonde, maybe five feet, curvy, dancing with her friends.

"She's cute, man. What're you doing over here with us?" I smile at him.

Martin shrugs. "I don't want to come on too strong, ya know? We've hooked up a handful of times. But I think I should play it cool."

I roll my eyes. "Why do people always say that? If you like her, make it known. Guys who play games rarely win, especially if the girl is as great as you say she is."

"Man, what do you know?" Rodney whines, because statistics girl has been flirting with another guy all night.

I lean farther back into the wall, smug because these tactics of love some guys play are just plain dumb. "And how's that going for you? You know, if you just go over and talk to her, you may hit it off. You may decide she's not your type. She may want to go home with you at the end of the night. But instead, you're going to stand over here, criticizing me."

"Yo, you guys have to see this!" Paul runs up to us, motioning us out of the room and into the grand hallway of this house we're in.

It's a typical college party house, the kind you see in movies. Enormous, probably housing at least ten or twelve guys, and it looks like a bunch of guys live here. There is barely any furniture, the fridges, three of them, are all filled with beer, and the entire place is set up for one thing: partying. There is also a grand staircase out of a Hollywood mansion when you walk through the front door, but of course, this one has a two-story beer bong set up and the walls are littered with posters of naked girls.

Above my head, jeers and shouts start. The crowd at the bottom of the stairs looks up, and a girl teeters there on the railing, all but falling over. She's probably going to smack her head on the floor below and crack it wide open, with how she's swaying over the bannister.

"Who dares me to ride it down?" she screams, and the voice hits my spine like ice water.

It's hazy and dark in here, but if I squint, I can make her out. Jolie.

Her legs dangle over the railing as she sits atop it, mile-high shoes strapped to her ankles. She's wearing a white scrap of cloth over her round, perky breasts, and an equally small piece of black cloth is barely covering her butt cheeks. All of those beautiful brown waves are thrown back as she laughs, and the air around her is as carefree as she is.

If she wasn't about to break her neck, I'd say she just about looks like the most gorgeous thing I've ever seen. She's mesmerizing, and she knows it, though she has no idea I'm standing in the crowd about to watch her attempt this drunken stunt.

And oh, is it ever drunken. The camp counselors would occasionally sneak bottles of liquor around a campfire on the Sunday switch-over when our cabins weren't filled with campers. But I never saw Jolie this crazy, this recklessly under the influence. Glancing around, and listening to some of the whispers rising up, this appears to be a typical thing.

People start to chant, *do it, do it, do it*. So she swings another leg over, and before my eyes, begins to ride down the bannister.

I calculate the distance, my eyes flitting back and forth between Jolie and the bottom of the stairs.

She's going to shoot right off the end of the bannister and into the wall. Her fate is decided in some kind of bone break, and as she starts to gain momentum, I'm throwing morons out of the way. My worry and panic is accompanied by the hyena laughs and shouts of encouragement from the idiots cheering her on, and I'm nearly at the bottom of the stairs as Jolie's momentum sends her off-kilter.

I watch it, her expression, as it changes from glee to fear. She knows what is about to happen. At the last moment, I fling my arms out, catching her. We go tumbling back, my shoes barely hanging onto the floor as her inertia rebounds into me. But I tighten my arms around her, refusing to let her fall or be hurt.

She gasps in my ear, her body going stock still, as my back finally collides with the wall. I forget that anyone else even exists around us as her eyes meet mine. There is a flicker of recognition through the haze of the alcohol she's consumed, and her lip turns down in a frown. It's not at me, but more at ... the situation? I wish I could take her outside, or somewhere private, and ask her why she does this kind of thing.

And then she's moved out of my arms, the limbs feeling empty without her in them.

"Good thing this dweeb was here." Some beefcake grabs her by the arm.

Jolie willingly stumbles into him, giggling and batting her eyelashes. "I can handle myself."

"Bet you can." He leers at her chest.

She's all but forgetting I'm standing here, or that I just saved her from a trip to the emergency room. Christ, what am I doing? Every time I go out of my way for this girl, she shows me just how much she appreciates it.

Which is zero.

Jolie Kenner is nothing but a selfish party girl looking for her next adrenaline rush. And if she wants to fail out of school, break bones in the process, or act like an idiot with guys who certainly don't respect her, then I am not going to get in the way anymore.

I walk away without a backward glance, and she must not care to even follow, because I don't hear her calling me or feel her pull me back to talk.

"Get your girls, or don't, but the sober bus is leaving," I tell the guys, who are standing there staring at me with their mouths hanging open.

"Don't think we're not talking about this." Martin nods his head like a stern father figure.

Yeah, I didn't think I'd get off the hook about this one. Too bad I have no intention of bringing up Jolie ever again.

My fingers twist the white straps of my bikini until they're tied tight and I'm able to flip onto my back without flashing the entire Salem Walsh University pool.

Christine and Maddy lie next to me on identical navy loungers, burning their skin the same way I am; as only girls in their twenties with no signs of wrinkles yet can do.

"Can you even believe that Kylie is a billionaire? Like, of course, she looks like that and has a buttload of money." Maddy pouts, lying on her stomach but propped up on her elbows reading some trash magazine.

Christine thumbs another page of her thriller, and I can practically feel her eye roll. "Her looks come from plastic surgery and her money comes from never having to struggle for anything. She didn't have to take out loans to go to college, save paychecks to buy clothes from Urban Outfitters, or fill her car with gas using her last twenty."

I keep my mouth shut, because I never had to do any of those things either. It sounded so cliché, but sometimes when Christine talked about rich people never struggling, I wanted to snap back at her. Sure, I didn't know what it was like to struggle for money, but I knew what it was like to be ignored. To be raised by nannies. To be sent to expensive camps during the summer because my parents would rather vacation in the South of France without me.

I knew what it was like to be unfairly judged simply because your parents had deep pockets. I'd had to hide a lot of myself from these two, even if they were my best friends. I never wanted Christine to talk about me the way she was talking about that celebrity now.

And not struggling just because you had money? If she only knew what I was going through. Yes, it was because of my own stupid actions, but money didn't solve all problems.

"Damn, he's a snack." Madison whistles low in her throat, interrupting my thoughts.

All three of us turn to look at the muscular back powering through the water. The swimmer strokes effortlessly, almost gliding across one of the Olympic lanes of the pool. He looks so out of place, considering most everyone, including the guys, are just here to flirt, show off, and see each other in little to no clothing.

"Jeez, he's like Michael Phelps," Christine exclaims.

"Or Ryan Lochte. He's hotter." Madison nods, never taking her eyes off the swimmer as he flips against the wall and swims back down the lane.

"But a liar," I add, because the guy did lie pretty badly.

Not that I'm one to be giving moral judgment about liars.

"He looks pretty tall. I would give that a climb," Christine says appreciatively.

We all watch him as he swims, back and forth, back and forth, his hair glistening in the sun. There is something familiar about him—

Just then, he finishes his swim, pulling himself up out of the pool and not bothering with the steps or ladder. The muscles in his arms as he pushes up onto the concrete, the way his abs flex as he stands ...

Holy hell. It's Mick.

This moment, right here, is one of the most satisfying moments I've ever had. Because Christine and Madison are practically panting, and I can cross my arms and be smug. Not that they know what he is to me, but they are drooling over Mick. My Mick, the one that, at any other time I'd introduced him, they would have called nerdy and not my type.

I've known all along how freaking sexy he is, not that it's the only thing that matters, but I mean, come on, it feels good to be doing the horizontal hula with a guy who is severely attractive.

Not to say I'm not drooling just like my friends. With the way his auburn hair is slicked back off his face and the water is dripping off his lean but chiseled body. And those swim trunks are swollen in a particular area, one that sports the biggest cock I've ever seen. Everything south of my waist begins to tingle, because I know just how well he can use it. Christ, I'm so turned on by this guy.

"Wait a minute. Isn't that the guy who stopped you from almost breaking your neck the other night?" Maddy lowers her sunglasses.

"What?" I guffaw, because I sincerely have no idea what she's talking about.

Christine rolls her eyes, her big straw hat not obstructing them at the moment. "Of course, you don't remember. Were you that blackout? You decided it'd be funny to slide down the stair bannister, and basically almost busted your face into the hardwood floor. If Michael Phelps over there hadn't helped you, you'd have been in an ambulance."

"Wait, isn't he also the same guy we saw in the Pub? The one you hugged?" Madison points out, and I really want to drown her in that pool.

"I don't—" I'm about to throw them off the scent, but Christine is already hooked on it.

"Actually, yeah ... you're right. Who is he, Jolie?"

They're both staring at me, but all I can process is that Mick was at that party the other night, and came to my rescue. That was the second time since he showed up at Salem Walsh that he'd done that. First, with the tutoring, and now this? And both times, he'd had absolutely no reason to. Now even less than before, with all of those flippant words I'd said and how I'd treated him.

I've always been looking for the perfect Prince Charming, and the truth is, he's right in front of me. Except Mick is a brainiac wrapped in tinfoil instead of suits of armor, and hell, isn't that just the most romantic thing you ever heard?

He deserves so much more than what I've been giving him. He deserves apologies, better treatment. He deserves better than me.

Still, I can't let this go on for one more second. "I have to go."

I grab my bag, pull on my hat, and start running after Mick, who is halfway down the sidewalk outside the pool now.

"Mick!" I yell, trying to catch up with him.

He doesn't turn, and I don't know if it's because he doesn't hear me or because he's choosing not to. Either way, I trail him, my flip-flops smacking the pavement.

When I get close enough, I grab his elbow, stopping his progress. "Hey, Mick."

An annoyed sigh flairs his nostrils. "What do you want, Jolie?"

His iciness takes me back a bit. "Um ... I just ... saw you back there at the pool."

"And what, didn't want to come to say hi with your friends right there?" Hurt flickers in his stunning green eyes.

My heart blanches. "No, I didn't realize it was you until one of them pointed out the swimmer. I would have said hi, but my friends were too busy drooling over you."

That compliment doesn't even faze him. "Okay."

I blink, knowing he's about to walk away any second. "I'm ... thank you for the other night. And I'm sorry. I feel so embarrassed, and I would have called sooner to thank you—"

"But you were so blackout drunk that you didn't remember." He finishes for me.

The shame in my cheeks is a hot, glowing red. "Yes."

There is nothing else I can say. I had no idea it even happened, that I'd done something so dangerous. It doesn't surprise me, I've seen the videos and heard the stories of what I do when I've had too much liquor and can't remember. It's never made me question myself before this, but with Mick standing there like an ugly, tarnished mirror, I can't help but feel ashamed. I promised myself I wouldn't do this anymore, that I'd get my head on straight and stop being so irresponsible. And yet, I'd just played right into that narrative the other night.

"I'm really sorry. I had a bad day, and I was just trying to cope with that. I ... uh, I failed my biology quiz."

Mick frowns, but doesn't say anything.

"Thank you, really. My friends said you basically saved me from a trip to the hospital. You've been so kind to me, and I've been a total bitch. I was horrible, Mick. I'm truly sorry."

I know words are just words, but I hope he can see the sincerity in my eyes.

"That's too bad about your quiz." I see a flicker of compassion on his face.

"Can I just take you out? For a meal, a drink? I want to make this up to you. I owe you something. Please, Mick, let me do something nice for you."

I see it in his eyes, the no that is right on the tip of his tongue. So I cut him off.

"Please. Let me take you to one of my favorite places in town. You haven't tasted fried catfish like this before."

He lets out a frustrated sigh. "Fine. But let me change. I can't very well wear a bathing suit to a restaurant."

I have to hold my tongue as he walks away, not knowing if he'll actually show up when I text him later, and wanting so badly to tell him I'll help get him out of that wet suit.

13

Why am I a sucker for this girl?

I'd all but sworn her off three nights ago, and now I'm sitting across from her at a restaurant. She got me with the catfish, and I don't know how she knew it was one of my favorite things to order on the rare occasion I got to go out for dinner.

I feel like a total moron, giving into her so easily. But when she said she failed her biology quiz, and I know it's because I wasn't tutoring her, and the predicament she's in well, my heart just caved. I'm an idiot, I know it.

But the catfish does look really good.

We're sitting at some seafood shack right on the beach, about thirty minutes from Salem Walsh's campus, and it's picturesque. The waves are just feet from our rusted, cracked, wooden picnic table, and the whole place smells like salt and fish-fry. The sun is slowly descending in the sky, not sunset colors yet but close to it, and I'm sipping on the freshest lemonade I've had in well, maybe ever.

"It's good, right? Like really good?" Jolie looks at me expectantly, hoping that I give her any shred of acknowledgment for bringing me here.

I've been pretty cold thus far, denying her request to pick me up and instead taking my own car. I don't need to be stuck in the same front seat on the ride back if things get awkward. And what kind of guy wants the girl to pick him up anyway? It's bad enough that Jolie won't introduce me to her friends, I don't need her chauffeuring me to dinner. I say dinner, because this is definitely not a date.

"Yeah, it's good." I turn my head toward the waves.

"Are you thinking about trying out for the swim team?" she asks, eagerly trying to start a conversation.

I don't look at her. If I look at her, I'll have to admire the pretty short-sleeved white sundress she's wearing, and things won't end well for me. She's too beautiful against even my hardest heart.

"No, it just helps me clear my head." Because it does.

I don't have time to join a sports team in college, with all my time being designated for my studies. And even if I did, I don't feel like getting competitive. I did it in high school because it looked good on college applications, before I realized I'd be going to community, and the jealousy and positioning for spots was always way too dramatic for me. I swim now because it helps me to get out of my own mind about all the worries and stress in my life.

"Got it, makes sense. I wish I could swim as well as you, it's really something to watch. I remember those relays this summer, you smoked everyone." She chuckles to herself.

The memory has me biting back a smile, because I remember how terrible of a swimmer she is. "And you all but doggy-paddled and drowned."

Jolie surprises me when she cracks up. "God, I'm a shit swimmer, it's true. Apparently, I didn't get the Phelps skills that you did."

We're interrupted by the waitress as she sets down plastic baskets full of fried catfish and hand-cut salt and vinegar potato chips. They smell divine, and I swear, my mouth begins to water.

"Did you know that catfish is my favorite dish?" I ask out of curiosity.

Jolie picks up her cutlery without looking at me. "You mentioned it one night this summer, and I remembered."

I honestly don't even remember mentioning that and am surprised she pulled that out of nowhere to coerce me into eating with her.

"Were you just holding that one up your sleeve until you really needed it?" I smirk at her.

Jolie reads me right, that I'm only half being serious, and grins. "Perhaps."

We dig in, and holy hell, she's right. This is the best catfish ever.

"I know." Jolie sighs, seeming to read my thoughts.

"How did you find this place?" I ask, because it really isn't on the beaten path.

The beach located near Salem Walsh has a boardwalk attached to it, with bars and seaside eateries and even a small amusement park. But Jolie didn't bring us there. This little shack is miles down, in a residential part of town.

She shrugs. "I like looking for unique restaurants and found this on a Yelp board when I was looking up something else near campus one day. It's my little secret, so don't go sharing it with just anyone. I don't need this place overrun by students."

I hold up three fingers, as if to show her on scout's honor that I won't reveal it to everyone I know.

As we eat, we keep catching each other's eyes. The quiet, the smell of the ocean, the easy ambiance ... it kind of reminds me of our summer together. Maybe we just do better this way, away from reality, in a pretty location, where who we are doesn't matter. It's when we're out in the real world that stuff gets complicated.

When she sets down her napkin, patting her stomach, she finally looks at me straight on.

"I really am sorry, Mick. I've lived in my own selfish world for a long time. When I came to college, it wizened me up a bit, but camp showed me a whole new side of the world. Of being responsible for something other than yourself. And when you look at me, I feel like I can be something better than I am. I've been doing well, I swear, but I just backslid that night. And then apparently decided to slide some more, right down that banister."

She gives a sheepish grin, because she gave a serious apology but tossed in some humor.

I chew over that information in my mind, because I don't want to say anything rash. "I appreciate that—"

"And if it makes a difference, I'd love for you to come over to my house to meet my friends. I think they'd really like you. Even if it's just to introduce you as my friend. They kind of know what I did this summer, but we could tell them all about it." Her voice is rushed, as if she's making up for how poorly she's treated me already.

Right there, Jolie is making it known that she would still want to be ... something. I can't help but wonder if, because her friends ogled me at the pool, I'm now suddenly acceptable to bring home. The thorn of being the nice guy, the nerdy guy, needles at my side, a constant pain for me.

"I was going to say that I really appreciate it, and I'm happy you're trying to be better. But there is a lot you don't know about me, Jolie. A lot of things that complicate my life, and I just don't have room for anything else in it. I had a lot of fun this summer, and it's been a nice surprise seeing you. Sometimes." I chuckle, because we both know some of the other times haven't been pleasant. "But right now, I just have to focus on my studies. I don't mind tutoring you again, because I'd love to see you succeed, but as for anything more than that, I just don't have the time. I don't mean that in an offensive way, I just need to focus on my goals right now."

Jolie looks down at her plate, smiling and shaking her head. "Only you can reject a girl and make it sound like the nicest, most sincere thing ever."

"I do mean it. I'm glad I agreed to come here tonight, I think we had some things to hash out. I'm never one to really hold a grudge, life is short. But that shortness also means I have places I want to go, and so I have to see those through."

Jolie nods, her eyes pensive as she looks out to the ocean. "I can understand that. But I'm still going to consider us friends. And if you ever need a friend to listen about those complications, I'm here."

That statement hits me like a ton of bricks. Jolie can't know what she just offered because no one has ever offered that to me before. Maybe because I've never given anyone the chance to. I don't let anyone in on the pain, the heartache of my life.

Could I ever do that? Probably not.

But now I know if I need to, there is a girl, that in any other circumstance or lifetime I'd give my right leg to be with, offering her shoulder to lean on.

14

I may be a great student, an ardent studier and a general rule follower.

Many things that make me a perfectionist, or some kind of accurately programmed robot. No, seriously, some of the kids in high school called me a robot. And I'm okay with all of that, I just wish it came with one thing.

A better affinity for being a morning person. It seems oxymoronic that I'm geeky, love education and schooling, barely have a social media presence, and possess all the other traits for acting like a middle-aged father when I'm only twenty-one, yet cannot drag myself from bed before seven thirty a.m. And even then, it's with a scowl and a desire for an entire pot of coffee.

My mom always joked that you couldn't safely talk to me until at least nine a.m., and I'm pretty sure my homeroom teacher in high school used to rib me and say that instead of getting the worm like the early bird, I ate it.

It's a personality trait I just can't change, no matter how hard I try. I've gotten up at six a.m. to go swim, tried the whole journaling thing, even did meditation for a month or two. Nothing helps. I'm just not a morning person, and I have to face it.

But right now, I'm fighting through the annoyance that I'm not still in bed, because the early bird might not get the worm in my book, but he could score an internship.

I got it on good advice, from a professor I'd particularly bonded with, that Dr. Richards likes to go into his laboratory early on Wednesday mornings to research, theorize, and come up with experimental possibilities. So here I am, at six a.m., armed with the notebook I've been scribbling ideas in since my dad got sick, at the auxiliary medical campus for Salem Walsh University.

The hospital that borders campus on its right side is a state-of-the-art facility. I've read many research papers and journals, not all of them on ALS, that have come out of the operating rooms and laboratories in that building. Most guys worships sports heroes, but I worship scientists. My quarterbacks and MVPs are right through those doors, and as I push past them, I'm met with a feeling of reverence.

The hospital is quiet this time of morning, and I enter from the clinician side, so there are no patient visitors milling about. My professor with insider knowledge spelled out to me how to get to the laboratory, and told me that if Dr. Richards gets pissed that I crashed his quiet time, not to mention his name.

Making my way through the halls and snaking past rows of rooms, all dark and quiet, I finally make it to a door that's light shines through the small window in it. When I peek through, I see someone sitting at the bank of sleek computers, a micro-scope sitting next to him, as well as several other high-tech looking machines.

I push through the door, and his head flies up, turning to watch as I enter.

"Dr. Richards, good morning."

The man looks up, his gray stubble and shock of white hair

blending in with his lab coat. "How did you get in here? This laboratory is closed at this time of morning."

I hold up the hand that isn't clutching my notebook. "I know that, sir, and I apologize. I just wanted to come talk to you. I've been following your research for a very long time."

I think I might be scaring the guy, because his stool scrapes across the floor. "What is this?"

A nervous laugh pops out of my mouth, and I feel like a complete fanboy. Is this what people feel like when they meet a rock star?

"No, no. I ... jeez, I'm really screwing this up, huh? Okay, let me start over. My name is Mick Barrett, and I'm a junior biology student here at Salem Walsh. I have been following your ALS trials and research for years, and I wanted to personally come meet you."

Dr. Richards looks a little startled, but moves to me and reaches out a hand. "Well, good to meet you, then."

I shake it, and plunge forward, knowing that I'm going to be abrasive but not caring. "Very good to meet you. I was also wondering if there was any possibility of interning on your trials. In any capacity. I'll grab your coffee, clean the lab—"

Now he gives me a stern look, because people must try to do this kind of thing often. "Young man, there is a full application and vetting process for the interns who work in this lab, and they're usually second-year medical students. I appreciate your initiative, but please contact the intern coordinator for the hospital if and when you're accepted into the medical program."

It's dismissive, and I understand why, but I've taken no for an answer approximately zero times in my life. I'm always the type of person to keep pushing, to keep fighting for what I want.

"I appreciate all of that, Doctor, but I'm not going to wait. My father was diagnosed with ALS six years ago. In that time, I've been his full-time caregiver, that is until I came here at least. And I came here to help find a cure, that's my ultimate goal."

I hold out the notebook, my most precious possession. All of my musings, thoughts, theories and everything else is written on these pages.

"You don't owe me anything. No one does. Believe me, I've learned that lesson tenfold. But if you could just take this, read through it, I think you'll see that I could bring something to this laboratory. You may say I'm too close to the whole thing, that my personal ties will affect my work. I call bullshit. If anything, it only makes me work harder. Please, just read through it. If ... if you think it's worth anything, my name, phone number, and email address are inside the front cover. Again, I'd do anything to be an intern here, even memorizing your Starbucks order."

Dr. Richards just nods, but I understand it's my time to go. I walk out with my head held high, counting this as a victory. He could have thrown the notebook back at me, scoffed in my face as a junior with absolutely no medical degree.

As I exit the hospital doors, the morning sun glints in my face and the air smells fresh. Maybe those morning birds are onto something, because this time of day is pretty nice, I guess.

I'm halfway to the Pub, to grab myself a coffee or seven, when my phone rings.

"Mom?" I don't even bother saying hello.

There is no reason a parent should call their college student at seven a.m. unless they completely forgot time etiquette, or something was wrong.

"Hi honey, I don't want you to worry ..."

If you ever call someone and tell them not to worry in the first sentence of the conversation, expect them to go into a full-blown panic.

"What's wrong?" I ask, my voice reaching a note it hasn't since my thirteenth birthday.

Mom pauses, and I can hear her talking to someone else. "Dad had a fall today. We're at the hospital, but he's doing fine, sweetheart. Really. I just wanted to call and tell you, before you called the house and began worrying when we didn't pick up. I know how you get ... diligent."

She's saying this because if she or the aides don't pick up within one or two phone calls, I will start ringing them off the hook. It took a lot for me to go away to college, even if it's just three hours in easy traffic away from home. As the primary caregiver for my dad for the last couple of years, it's beyond difficult to give up control of his treatment. To be out of the loop, out of the picture, for a lot of things. Not only does his diagnosis interest me, but it consumes me. The science and the love I have for him are completely intertwined, and I have a hard time letting go of that anxiety.

He's my father, I wish like hell I didn't have to be talking about this. I wish like hell that he wasn't sick, that I could be like every other normal college student and worry only about when the next party was and if I was making it to class on time.

"He fell? Where? How? What the hell happened?"

"Calm down, honey, he's all right." Mom's voice is meant to infuse calm, but my pulse ratchets higher and higher. "He was at the gym with a new trainer, since Bethenny is on vacation. The temporary trainer is versed in helping strength train those with illnesses or disabilities, but he turned his back for a second and Dad was poised the wrong way on a piece of equipment. He fell and couldn't catch himself, obviously. Internally, there is nothing wrong. Just a gash on his nose which they had to stitch up, and then some minor scrapes and bruises on his hands and arms. He's fine, sweetheart."

My heart is beating so rapidly, it's a wonder it's not breaking free of my ribcage. I feel like one of my lungs has collapsed, that's how hard it is to breathe.

"I'll drive home, I could be there by noon. I'll tell my professors what happened—"

"Mick James Barrett, stop it. You are not coming home. Dad will be fine. I can have him FaceTime you later, as he's sleeping peacefully right now after the events of the morning."

"But he'll know I'm not there, and I have to talk to his trainer—"

"Mick. Please." Mom is begging me, I can hear it in her voice. "What your father and I want for you right now is to be a normal college kid. To stop worrying about such adult problems. We're so proud of what you're doing there, and you've spent way too much of your life stressing about things that Dad and I should be able to handle. Be a kid, Mick. Be a little reckless. Don't study all the time. We're so proud of you, but you deserve some fun."

She says that, but we both know I won't follow through on it. My window for fun passed long ago, and the summer was the only time I gave myself permission to let the control slip a little bit. Now it was back to the straight and narrow.

"Okay, Mom. Call me when he wakes up, okay?" I ignore her request for me to be a normal kid.

"Okay, bud. I love you."

"Love you, too," I say, before hanging up.

Why does this always happen to me? It feels like I have one small victory, and then the universe slaps me back down again. Do I not deserve just one day, even one hour, of feeling happy? Of not worrying about all of the crap that is typically rained down upon me?

I skip my morning coffee, instead deciding to head back to the dorms. I'm never one for a nap, but I don't have a class until ten and I'm freaking exhausted to my bones.

My theory has proven correct; I knew getting up before the crack of dawn can lead to nothing but trouble.

15

A week goes by and I have my first no-tension, friendly tutoring session with Mick.

We meet in the library, this time at a public table on the second floor, and go over cohesion and adhesion. Yet again, Mick explains the subject matter in a language I can understand, and I actually end up getting a ninety on the next quiz.

And even though I want to, I don't ask Mick anything personal or suggest we do anything other than study together. It pains me the entire time, since he looks edible in those fuck-me glasses and jeans that fit his ass in a way I've never seen on him before. The whole time, he seems preoccupied by something else, though he's as pleasant and nice as ever.

You know those people that other people always refer to as the nicest human they've ever met? That's Mick Barrett. He's just ... *good*. In a way that a lot of other people aren't, and never will be. He's the type of person that makes me want to be a better person.

I wonder every day about those complications he wouldn't tell me about. What's he got going on in his life that when he looks at me, I can tell those vibrant green eyes are in a completely different place?

That's what I'm pondering as the girls and I eat lunch, one I was late to again because of traffic between this campus and the community college one.

"Didn't you say you were in that Theories of Sexuality course?" Christine asks, focusing more on her roast beef sandwich than me.

I cough, focusing my eyes on my spicy tuna roll. "Uh yeah, it's super interesting."

"That's weird, because I mentioned to that girl Becky, who is in my major, that my best friend was taking the class. You remember meeting her a couple times? She said she didn't see you in there."

My heart ices over with sheer panic. This is the moment I've been waiting for, the one where the other shoe drops. I can keep lying, or I can own up to the truth. I don't know why I'm hiding it from them; I think my friends would be supportive. If anything, they'd probably feel bad since they too ran from the fountains that night.

But it's ingrained in me. This need to appear like the perfect, carefree it-girl. Nothing bad happens in my life, that's what I was always taught to portray. The ugly, terrible things we did were swept under the carpet or neatly arranged behind the curtains. And I also don't want to see the pity in their eyes; something about being vulnerable with people has always unnerved me. It's bad enough that Mick knows my secret, I wake up in a cold sweat some nights just wondering what he truly thinks of me because of my current predicament.

So I take a chance. "Really, that's weird? Well, it's a big lecture."

I have no idea if it's a big lecture or not, I'm just sending that one out as a Hail Mary.

"Hmm, I thought that one was only fifty people?" Madison says, as if she knows.

"That's still a lot of people in there," I argue, starting to feel the sweat dripping down my neck. "Wait, which class is that?"

Christine rolls her eyes. "You can never remember your schedule. It's Tuesday and Thursdays at two p.m."

I snap my fingers, lying on the spot. "Oh, you know what? She may have forgotten, because I wasn't there last class. Yeah, walked in, and immediately felt that familiar rush. Aunt Flow time, if you get what I mean."

Madison groans. "Ugh, I hate when that happens. It's like your whole week is going well, and then there is suddenly blood in the water."

"Shark week." Christine giggles.

"Yes!" I slap my knee, as if this period emergency was really serious. "I had to go back to the house, rummage around for a tampon, and all we had were pads. So by that point, I figured I'd call it a day. Went to the store, picked up tampons and a pint of ice cream. It was medicine, really."

They both nod gravely.

"You deserved it. I remember this one time, I had a tampon fall out of my purse in middle school. I was mortified. All of these boys saw it, and I lied and said I had to go to the nurse to go home. Can you imagine? Now I'm like, shit, if you want to have sex on my period, I'm all for it." Christine shrugs.

"You like period sex? I've always found it so messy." Madison looks mildly grossed out.

"I'll only do it with someone I've been seeing or hooking up with for a while," I add, not feeling one way or the other. "If it's a new guy, definitely no. You gotta give them the best version of the ... puss."

My girlfriends crack up, and I'm just glad we're not on the hot topic of my class schedule anymore.

"I agree. If I'm not freshly shaved with some sprays of perfume down there, I'm not offering it up." Madison bites into one of her pieces of grilled chicken as if this is nuclear science we're talking about.

"As if you don't shave clean before we go out every single night of the weekend." Christine rolls her eyes.

I hold my hand up. "Hey, you never do know when a hot guy will come your way. You have to be prepared."

"But if you're prepared, then you're always going to be DTF. And sometimes, that's just desperate." Christine steals one of my pieces of sushi off my plate and pops it in her mouth.

"Did you really just say DTF? That makes it sound way sluttier than anything." I chuckle, laughing at her use of the acronym for *down to fuck*. "Not that I think being ready to go at any moment is desperate or slutty. Listen, I enjoy sex. I enjoy it with different partners, or the same one for a while. I like experimenting, and it makes you feel good. I don't see how that could ever be a bad thing. Wrap it up, be safe, and be prepared at all times to get naked and freaky."

Madison starts clapping. "Amen, girl. Yes!"

Christine has a different opinion, and we all know it, so she keeps her mouth shut about that, but pipes up about period sex.

"Whatever. I'm just saying, I don't want to get menstrual blood all over a random stranger's penis."

I make a barfing noise. "Okay, we're *eating*."

"Let's talk about the biggest penis you've ever seen!" Madison pipes up, and I'm pretty sure the table next to us is definitely listening to our conversation.

My mind flashes back to Mick, and I'm momentarily sad that I probably won't ever see it again. Or get to play with it.

Madison starts chattering on about cocks and piercings, and I'm just relieved that the talk of my course schedule has turned into sex talk.

16

The Salem Walsh Campus Center is packed full of students, tickets dangling from their fingers.

I wait in line, flutters of excitement moving through my stomach at the prospect of getting to see this show. One great part of being at a top-notch university is that musical acts and comedians make tour stops at your school.

Anthony Render, one of my favorite comedians, was put on the schedule of events at Campus Center a month ago, and I'd woken up at six a.m. to grab my ticket online. None of the other guys in my dorm suite got tickets, because they'd woken up too late, but I'm okay with going alone. It's going to be a relaxing night off for me, one where I can laugh and put my problems aside for an hour or two.

After I get my ticket scanned, I head into the Campus Center Arena. It's a big theater where all the touring acts perform, and the whole place is draped in navy and gold.

The seating is first come, first serve in the four-thousand-seat arena, and I carefully make my way around the people lining up for the first row. Have they ever been to a comedy show? Don't they know that the people in the front row are often the ones being made the butt of the joke by the comedian? I love Anthony Render's jokes, but I'm going to pick a seat about eight rows back, in the corner, where he can't see me and make fun of the covalent bonds pun shirt I'm wearing.

Jolie and I see each other at the same time, as we enter the row from different sides, and both do a double take.

"Hi," she says, seeming kind of stunned.

"Uh, hi," I say, my feet moving me toward her because there are other people trying to come into the row.

She entered from the empty side, and must have walked all the way around to get a seat closer to the far wall. What I'm most surprised about is the fact that she appears to be alone.

"Are you, do you need these seats for people?" I ask, pointing to the one directly next to her as we stand there awkwardly.

Jolie shakes her long brown mane. "Nope, just me."

"Oh," I say.

We're basically standing in front of the last two seats available in the row, and how weird is it that fate brought us to these two seats at this moment? I could have picked anywhere else in the arena to sit, as could she. I find it strange she's even here to see this comedian, but maybe she just likes to come to campus events.

"Should we ... do you care if we sit next to each other?" she asks.

There have been three study sessions total since we went out to the seafood shack, and they've been nothing but behaved and platonic. We usually meet for about half an hour in the library, go over her workbooks or packets, and then part ways. We haven't texted aside from meetup times, and I've not attended any more parties where I have to save her from breaking her neck.

Each time we're together, I know we're both edging away from the cliff of suggesting we hang out more. But now we're here, and it would be extremely awkward to refuse to sit next to her. We'd have to shuffle our way out of the row, and it's … harmless. It's just a seat. Right?

"Yeah, sure." I sit down, adjusting my wallet in my back pocket.

Jolie sits next to me, her familiar scent wafting my way as she sticks her purse under her chair. Per usual, I have to actively try to stop checking her out. She has on this long-sleeve shirt with a V-neck, and when she bends a certain way, I can see right down into her cleavage. I'm not that guy, the one who leers, but with Jolie, I can't help it.

"Do you like this comedian?" she asks politely.

I nod. "He's one of my favorites. Can't believe I get to see him as a student for free. How about you?"

"Oh, I love Anthony Render. One of my friends from home got us tickets to see his stand-up routine in New York two years ago, and I've been obsessed ever since."

I remember watching that special on Comedy Central. "Wow, you were at that show?"

"Yeah, he's just hilarious. I wasn't going to pass up the opportunity to come see him. My friends weren't interested, so figured I'd come alone." Jolie pauses. "I'm kind of glad I did. Gives us a chance to hang out."

The way she says it, in that shy, cautious way, makes my heart crumble. This is not a woman who is hesitant or unsure about almost anything. She's confident and brash. Knowing that I make her feel the same way she makes me feel is … well, it makes my stomach dip.

Jolie chuckles a little, but says nothing.

"What?" I ask.

"It's nothing. Just think it's funny that we both like this comedian. I mean, I know a lot of other people love him, too, but you and I don't have much in common. It's nice to discover something that we *do* have in common."

I hadn't thought about this before. "I guess that's true. Although, for the record, we don't have to have things in common. I still like you as a person."

Jolie turns her full gaze to me then, her expression unreadable. We just look at each other, probably for too long, but I can't stop.

We're saved by Anthony Render, who is announced at the exact moment Jolie looks like she's about to say something. The lights go down and he comes onstage, so we turn our attention that way.

As we sit next to each other, my elbow on the armrest and her hand on her thigh, I can't help but feel the energy between us. It's electric, radiating off the sides of our bodies. It feels like at any moment, a static spark could explode without us even touching. I swear, I can hear Jolie's breathing increase, my own coming out in labored puffs. I have to adjust, because for some reason, my cock has risen to attention.

Maybe it's that it's dark in here, or that she's so close I can almost feel the hairs on her arms. Either way, I'm one second from letting the words off the tip of my tongue. Of suggesting we get out of here, because if she clears her throat again in that sexy, groaning way, I'm going to rip her shirt off right here in this audience.

I try to focus on the comedy show, I really do, but all my brain seems to want to address is Jolie's body being inches from mine. She starts drumming her hand on her thigh, and ... did she just squirm?

I'm doomed.

It seems like hours that I sit here, trying to calm my wildly beating heart and talk my penis under control. Finally, when the lights come up, a bit of the spell is broken, but neither of us moves as the crowd begins to empty out.

"That was really funny," she says, scooting to the edge of her seat but not standing.

"He's great," I agree, sitting up straighter, but also not standing.

A beat passes, and I feel myself falling into her. Her familiarity, the way I feel around her, how she keeps surprising me. I don't want this to end, and actually had a better time tonight than I have in, well, since we spent the summer together.

"Do you—" I begin, but Jolie cuts me off.

"Well, I should probably get home. I have another biology quiz tomorrow, and we both know how much I need to pass." She laughs quietly.

She made the decision for both of us, stomping on the embers that were building. It's for the best, I know that, but I can't help the disappointment that sits in my gut. Jolie is only following the boundaries I've set in place. And they're necessary. But for a split-second, I wish they weren't.

"Yeah, I should get back, too." I nod in agreement. We both stand, facing each other. "Well, good luck on your quiz tomorrow."

It feels like I should lean in, maybe brush a kiss on her cheek or give her a hug. But that would be so far over the line I've put between us, and I have to physically plant my feet to the floor.

Then we walk to opposite sides of the row. And I'd be a liar if I said I didn't turn back to see if she had too.

"Thanks for coming over, I just had to wait here for the repair guy."

I usher Mick into my off-campus house, and it's strange that he's standing here, in my living room. He's so tall that the ceilings seem lower, and from the moment he stepped inside just now, that familiar buzz started between us.

"No problem, I didn't realize you were so close to campus," he says, looking around our ranch.

I want to know what he sees from his eyes. It's a cozy place, with a beige sectional couch Christine's parents let us take to school and a flat-screen TV my dad bought us. From the small living room, it opens up into the kitchen, with the counters littered with our diet food and alcohol. From there a hallway shoots off, where three small but single bedrooms are.

"Welcome to our humble abode. It's not much, but it serves its purpose." I wave a hand around.

Mick nods, and I think we're both aware that we're alone in a quiet house. "It's nice. Better than a loud dorm and a communal bathroom."

I cringe. "I forgot those days. We've only been here for a

couple of months, and I wouldn't go back for a million dollars. How many roommates do you have?"

"Four. They're cool, though. It's better than my parents' house and commuting to community college." Mick fiddles with the backpack on his shoulder.

"Wait, you went to community college?" My jaw practically unhinges at his words.

Mick's eyes twinkle with taunting. "Yeah, didn't I mention that?"

"You most definitely did not! Here I was, feeling like a total fuckup compared to the genius future scientist tutoring me, and all along you were in the same position! You went to community before you transferred here? Why?"

It's not like he couldn't have gotten into any of the top colleges. Jesus, Mick had probably gotten a perfect score on the SATs.

He shrugs. "I had family stuff at home. I couldn't leave, so I enrolled at the community college until I could."

It's the only other time he's mentioned those problems and secrets he has to focus on, and I don't want to ask what they are. If he wants a shoulder, he'll lean on mine, and clearly he doesn't.

"I didn't realize that. You must be glad to be here."

"You have no idea," he mutters, and a part of me hopes he's not just talking about Salem Walsh.

But that he's talking about my house.

We for sure almost slept together the other night. If either one of us had been a little more bold, or I'd had one sip of wine, we would have been back at one of our places, screwing each other's brains out.

"When is this repair guy supposed to get here?" he asks, breaking the tension.

I look at my phone. "He said between five and eight, and of course both my roommates had clubs going on, so I'm stuck here. Thanks for coming to study, we just need our washer and dryer fixed."

"Wouldn't want to mess up your laundry schedule." His deep voice worms its way between my thighs.

I physically shake my shoulders and try to talk myself out of trying to jump his bones. "So, should we start?"

Walking into the kitchen, I feel Mick following me, and my skin tingles. I'm so on edge, that when we start taking out our supplies and notebooks, I jump up.

"If we're talking about meiosis, I need a drink. You're having a drink with me," I tell him, not taking no for an answer. "It's been a hell of a day already, what with the broken appliances. You can't say no."

Mick seems to pause, and then holds up his hands, relenting. "Fine. But no tequila. And no beer."

Tapping my finger to my chin and surveying the liquor lineup on the counter, I make a decision. "How about the most gentlemanly drink of all? A gin and tonic?"

"Fine." Mick gives me a small smile.

I mix and pour our first drinks, handing him a plastic tumbler and clinking my cup against his. From there, we study, going over the most boring subject of all educational subjects. I'm retaining the information, but only because Mick is such a good teacher.

An hour later, we're two drinks in, and everything he says, I'm giggling at.

"Chromosomes are not funny!" Mick says, finishing the dregs of his drink. "This is how we make up what sex a person is born as."

A very unflattering snort bursts past my lips. "You said sex."

Mick chuckles, his eyes a little drunk. "You're right. I did. Can you please focus, Jolie?"

"Gosh, this is just so boring. Let's have another drink!" I clap my hands, standing to get the gin.

"No, we're not having another drink. I have to drive home after this, and I'm probably going to opt for walking as it is," Mick admonishes me.

And then I get an idea. It's probably a bad idea, since it makes my heart scorch and the very core of my belly melt with lust.

"Well, what if we up the stakes?" I say in a flirty, sexy tone.

He sits back, crosses those brawny, lean arms. "What does that mean?"

"If you're not going to let me have another drink, then I need another incentive. So, for every answer I get right, you have to remove a piece of clothing."

It's bold of me, and I'm going against everything Mick and I agreed upon. That we should be strictly friends, that we have other problems to focus on. But I'm tipsy, and horny, and I miss him. Of all the guys I've been with, he's hands down the best, and I miss *sex*, too.

Mick's emerald orbs flash, and I know he's considering it. His rational brain is screaming no, but the two gin and tonics and me leaning toward him, flashing my cleavage have the thing below his waist screaming yes.

"Jolie. We shouldn't ..." he says quietly.

"And yet, I think we definitely should." I nod my head vigorously. "Give me a term, come on, quiz me."

His eyes never leave mine. "What is a telomere?"

I have to dig deep into my brain, but it comes to me. "Special, essential DNA sequences at both ends of each chromosome."

Mick clicks his tongue. "You're right."

"Take it off, baby," I taunt him.

He bends down and comes up with a shoe. "Happy?"

"*Boooo*. That's a lame start. You could have begun with the shirt." I give him a thumbs-down.

"You have to earn that." And the flirty side of my summer fling rears its attractive head.

This guy is so fucking good-looking. Most would simply not see it, because it's not obvious. He's not a jock or a pretty boy. No, Mick's good looks are the kind that sneak up on you, but once you see them, you can't turn away. He's gorgeous in that unique, model kind of way. Seriously, this guy could be gracing the runways of Milan while my football friends are flexing their muscles at a frat party.

I get his next question correct too, and off comes the other shoe. Two socks later, and I know he's about to stop throwing me softballs.

"What is the difference between a diploid and a haploid?" Mick squares his jaw, thinking he has me.

Shit, he might have stumped me. My brain feels fuzzy from the drinks, and from the anticipation of possibly seeing him shirtless. I have to close my eyes.

"A haploid cell is a cell with chromosomes that come in homologous pairs. Homologous just means similar, but not identical. A diploid cell is a cell that has only one representative of each chromosome pair."

I hold my breath, and when he smiles like the devil, I know I'm wrong. "Nope. You had the definitions right, but unfortunately, you switched the terms. Diploids come in homologous pairs. Haploids only have one representative chromosome pair."

"Fuck," I mutter, snapping my fingers. "Okay, give me another one."

"I think you should have to take something off. It's only fair." Mick raises an eyebrow, leveling me.

Can't argue with Mr. Logic over there. Never one to shy from a dare, I pick a big piece of clothing, just to show him up. My fingertips reach for the hem of my shirt, and slowly, I pull it over my head. While the material blocks my view of his face as it passes over my eyes, my skin tingles knowing he's watching me.

I toss it to the side when it's off, sitting in nothing but a bra across the table from him.

If someone lit a match in here, the whole place would ignite.

We're staring at each other like feral animals, Mick's eyes on my tits and my breath coming out in labored puffs.

"I should ask you another question." He gulps.

I nod. "Yeah."

In the next beat, we're lunging for each other, chair legs scraping across the floor and our mouths crashing in the middle.

18

We're climbing over the table to get to each other.

One second, we were sitting there, wading through a minefield of study questions and strip dares, and the next, we were kissing like our lives depended on it.

Jolie's tongue is in my mouth, and I give it right back to her, kissing her with such fervor that I think there might actually be sparks coming off of us. My hands mold to her bare torso, skating up and over her velvet skin to cup the lacy, hot pink bra she wears. My thumbs dig down into the half-moons, finding her nipples and circling them with the blunt tips of my fingers.

She moans into my mouth, and if I wasn't already rock hard, I am now. Standing, never detaching our mouths, I take her with me. I don't want this table between us; I need to feel her pressed against me.

Once we're standing, Jolie begins to move us down the hall which I can only assume leads to her bedroom.

It's dumb, so dumb to be doing this. But I don't care. I'm too deep now, my erection standing at full mast and all the warning signs chucked out the window.

As we stumble past doors, our clothes come off. My shirt, her bra, my belt buckle, her leggings pushed down past her hips. By the time we make it to her room, which I barely get a chance to look around, we're half naked and my fingers are lodged inside her.

I remove them from pumping in and out of her as I push her gently on her bed, onto her back. And once her underwear is thrown behind me, I feast.

"Mick!" Jolie sobs out as soon as my lips latch to the sensitive, engorged bud between her thighs.

Jesus, I've missed the taste of her. And the sounds she makes when I scrape my teeth along her clit. Or how she squirms when I push my tongue inside her.

It all seems to be moving so fast, and yet so slow. I taste her endlessly, until she's gripping the sheets. Then Jolie is pulling me up by the shoulders and moving me onto my back as she removes my shorts and boxers along with them.

Then her mouth comes down over me, and I'm a goner. She bobs up and down, sucking me with such force and precision that I have to dig my nails into my palms to keep from coming.

"Condom," I choke, because her mouth on my cock may just cause me to stroke out.

Jolie sits up with a pop from her throat and it vibrates all the way down my shaft. She moves to her nightstand, pulling open the top drawer and producing a little foil packet. After handing it to me, she flips over onto her back.

As I roll the condom on, it occurs me to that this is our first time in a bed. During the summer, we had sex behind cabins, in sheds, on the floor of the barn, and in the woods. Never did I have her in my bunk, and she never brought me in hers. Probably because there were ten-year-olds within earshot, but still.

It's strange to be alone with her, in the most intimate place a person could have sex, no unforeseen obstacles or waiting to get caught.

Without another thought, I line myself up, dragging my protected tip from the top of her clit to the bottom of her slit. She lets out a ragged breath, and it's only then do I push in.

Her eyes flutter closed but mine are intensely trained on her face as I spread her legs wider.

"I've missed you," I murmur, not being able to get ahold of myself as my balls graze her ass.

"Yes." She loops her arms around my neck, opening her eyes.

Usually, we laughed or joked during sex, taunted each other. It was a fun, forbidden thing, and so we felt giddy during it.

Not this time. No, neither of us speaks. We simply stare, inhale the same breaths, and groan as I pump in and out of her. It feels … *more*. There's something underlying here, a massive thing building between us that no one in the room wants to put a name to. Maybe it's because we've let the sexual tension get so pent up. Maybe it's because we've spent time as friends this time, before tearing each other's clothes off.

Or maybe it has been here all along. And now that we know there could be a future past the end of August, it's planting its ideas and hopes in our hearts.

My cock twitches inside her as I go deeper, faster. I brace both hands next to her head, pushing up so that I can rail into her body.

I know she's coming without her ever having to say it. She mewls that familiar cry in the back of her throat, and then her nails scratch down my back as she arches.

Her face, that perfectly suspended bliss, is what tosses me over the edge. I grunt out my release as everything in me laser-focuses to the tip of my cock and I spurt into the condom.

We breathe into each other, my forehead against her

shoulder while I regain myself. When I can move, I flip over, pulling out of her and instantly feeling the warmth of her around me. My back hits the mattress, and I study the ceiling, trying to blink away the spots in my vision.

"That was ..." I breathe, unable to form thoughts.

Jolie doesn't say anything, and just as I'm about to look over to study her expression, the doorbell rings.

"*Shit*, that's the repair guy."

Jolie jumps up, hopping into her underwear and throwing on a random dress that hangs over the back of her desk chair.

"How do you know?" I ask, amused as I watch her jump around the room frantically.

"My roommates wouldn't knock, they have keys. Um ... hold on, okay?" She looks unsure as she leaves the room.

I lie in her bed, a queen that feels much larger than my twin, but my feet still hang off the end. The sheets are white and feel expensive under my back, and the furniture in here does not match the threadbare carpet and wood-paneled walls resurrected from the seventies. On the tack board above her desks are hundreds of pictures from dozens of places all over the world. I see her at the Eiffel Tower, in front of the Trevi Fountain, riding a camel in some desert. I knew before I saw these photos that we were vastly different, but this just puts a period on it.

My body is in bliss mode, and I know I should get up and get dressed, but it's the first ten minutes I've had all semester to chill and be in the moment. So I take it.

Listening to the muffled conversation out in the kitchen through Jolie's closed bedroom door, my cock starts to stiffen again thinking about what just happened. I should be freaking out more than I am, because I promised myself I wouldn't fall back into bed with her, but I'm not. It's probably those two drinks. Or my numbed-out post-orgasm brain.

Jolie slowly opens her door, coming back in with our discarded clothes in her hands. "So, uh, the repair guy is here ..."

She looks me up and down, and I see her eyes heat at the sight of my naked body. But there is also regret in those beautiful brown eyes.

"Should I go?" I ask.

A flicker of nausea hits my stomach, because the first thing I can think is that she doesn't want her roommates to see me.

"Um, I mean we could study in here? But I feel like we already completed the packet. What do you think?" she asks, leaving the decision up to me.

I sit up. "Yeah, I mean, it's getting late anyway. I should go."

"You don't have to if you don't—"

"No, it's fine—"

We both pause, looking sheepishly at each other.

"This isn't something you're going to regret, is it?" I ask, my honesty never knowing when to shut up.

Jolie comes to sit down beside me, her face breaking with relief. "No. I just ... we already talked about how we have a lot going on. We should ... keep this casual. I think the last thing either of us can handle right now is defining this. You have your goals, and I have mine. We should focus on those."

As much as what she's saying is logical, something I'm usually known best for, it still feels like she's slicing my heart open with little tiny stabs. Kind of like she's taking an envelope opener to it. Not enough to hurt if it's just one, but the sting grows unbearable as she slashes more and more.

"No, yeah, that makes sense." I nod my head, giving her my best poker face.

But those are things I said to her, and they do make sense. Except with what she just did, with the emotions neither of us can put words to, we just complicated things beyond belief.

"So, keeping things casual?" she asks, holding out a hand for me to shake.

I'm still naked, sitting in her bed, nothing casual about this. But I reach for her hand anyway. "Casual."

"Why is the best pizza place in town at the back of a gas station?"

Maddy asks this as she picks up her second slice of pepperoni, the grease dripping onto the plate.

"It's so true. Gross, but true." Christine nods as we sit at a rickety table in the back of Rowan's.

Technically, Rowan's is a gas station with a convenience store attached. But our freshman year they started serving pizza and fat sandwiches, or variations of sub rolls piled high with things like mozzarella sticks, cheesesteak, and french fries oozing with honey mustard. So while you sit there at one of the seven tables crammed into the side of the quickie mart, other students wander in to get a thirty rack of beer or candy bars to heal a roommate's broken heart.

We're splitting a pie, half pepperoni and half sausage, before getting ready for our Friday night party. And I'm celebrating. I passed another biology quiz—and I got laid this week.

It's been two days since I dragged Mick into my bedroom, and my mind has been swirling with it. Not to mention, our texting has picked up. It no longer only includes scheduling study meetups, but now details about our days, and flirty messages when the sun goes down.

What I really can't stop thinking about, though, is the look on his face when he left my house. It was disappointed, almost rejected, even though he'd just fucked me with the force of a thousand racehorses.

I said what I said to protect myself, and him. My heart was in that hookup way more than I bargained for. It felt like my chest cracked wide open when Mick stared down at me, as he was pushing himself inside me, connecting us. I could feel myself begin to melt in a way I never had, not even with him this summer.

The emotion was foreign and strange, and with no indication of how Mick feels, I have to nip it in the bud.

Plus, he has made it crystal clear before he started tutoring me again that he doesn't want anything more. Maybe he thinks falling back into bed together is a mistake, or doesn't want it to continue. He rejected me once, I can't risk my ego for that again.

And he shouldn't have to make that decision. He's already helped me pass biology thus far, and he's clearly got something going on back home. He doesn't need my problems, or the ones he won't tell me about.

It's as if my mind conjures him, because the bell over the door dings upon someone's arrival or exit. I look over my shoulder while Madison's eyes are glued to the sports update on the TV. She's the biggest female football fan I've ever met. Seriously, don't challenge her on her pigskin knowledge.

In walks a group of guys, all younger looking, with one sticking up out of the bunch. It takes me a minute, but I realize that Mick has just walked in with his roommates. Three guys, all in varying states of sweatpants, and then Mick is toward the back, wearing a sweatshirt with the solar system outlined on it.

He doesn't spot me, not until they're at the counter ordering, and when they sit down, it's clear he's here to stay. Should I introduce him to my roommates? Go over and say hi? We did say we were keeping it casual. Maybe I'll just see where he takes it.

Those eyes, the color of a seafoam ocean spray, connect with mine and Mick gives a slow, smiling nod. I return it, and my roommates don't see. Okay, so maybe he isn't expecting me to get up and go over. It doesn't look like he's doing the same.

Over the next half an hour, as we demolish our pizza and theirs is delivered to their table, I try to carry on the conversation with Christine and Madison. But with every passing second, I feel his gaze on my skin. I'm heated, and I wouldn't be surprised if I was blushing. More than too often, I sneak glances over my shoulders, smiling when we both slip up at trying to be sneaky.

It's a game we're playing, a flirty, secret game ... not unlike the one we played at Camp Woodwin. Mick's tongue darts out to wet his lower lip, I take a sip of my beer to cool myself down. It doesn't work, I still feel like I'm sitting on a volcano, my thighs squirming on the plastic chair.

My roommates discuss splitting a sundae to top it off and start discussing potential ice cream flavors. I can't take it any longer and need to go to the bathroom to splash cold water on my face.

"I'm going to the bathroom." I stand on shaky legs and make my way to the darkened hall at the back of the store.

It's quiet back here, cooler than the front of the building where Mick sits taunting me.

Except two seconds later, I hear footsteps behind me.

I whirl around, and there he is. That tall, lean body blocking the doorframe to the rest of the store.

"Hi," he says from the entrance of the hallway.

Those green eyes look me up and down, appreciating every inch.

"Hi to you." I nod, batting my eyelashes.

"How was your pizza?" he asks.

"Good. First time?" I say, and it's laced with so much more innuendo than pizza.

Mick shakes his head slowly, a cocky grin spreading on his lips. And before I know what he's doing, he grabs my elbow and pulls me into the bathroom.

It's a single stall, and even though someone is sure to come knocking, he locks the door behind my back before pinning me to it.

"I can't stop thinking about you." He breathes onto my lips as our noses touch.

My panties are wet in an instant, something so familiar and taboo about our secret meetings like this. It brings me back to the summer; of camp days and sneaking around.

"A quickie in a gas station bathroom? How desperate of us." I mean it to come off teasing, but it sounds more breathy on the end of a moan.

It's because Mick's fingers are flirting with the waistband of my jean shorts, and I want so badly to actually have that quickie I was taunting him about.

"Well, when you keep looking at me like that ..." he all but growls, planting a searing kiss on my lips.

I break it off. "Says the guy who was licking his chops at me."

He laughs sarcastically. "It was the pizza. It's just *that*. *Good*."

We both inhale and exhale at the same time, and then he seals his mouth to mine. The kiss is endless, slow and gentle but also intense and searching. My breath hitches in my throat when Mick pops the button on my shorts, sliding the zipper down.

For a moment, I think I hear a voice in the hallway, but it must be an employee, because no one comes knocking.

And then his fingers push past the elastic of my thong and

are up inside me. Mick muffles my cry as those two thick digits pump into my wet heat, causing me to spasm around them. I'm dangerously close to the edge already.

When he nips at my bottom lip, the bit of pain mixed with pleasure has my knees buckling. He doesn't take his mouth off of mine for one second, probably for fear that I'll have us both found out in this bathroom. That slight bit of worry that we may be caught is what's causing my orgasm to climb, I feed off the almost public nature of this.

Mick grounds his thumb into my clit, and I shoot off like a rocket. My whole body goes taut, my jaw slack, and I claw at his shoulders to keep myself upright. The waves course over me, and he doesn't stop pumping his fingers until I'm wrung dry.

In what might be the sexiest thing a man has ever done to me, Mick zips my shorts back up and then buttons them. His hands ghost over my hips, as if he's kissing them with his fingers.

"Come out to this party with us tonight," I say, still in the haze of my orgasm, not asking but not telling.

Mick shrugs. "It's not my scene."

"Yeah, but you could have me on the dance floor. And in my bed later tonight."

It goes against keeping it casual, making a plan to attend a party together, but I want more of what he just gave me. I want more of him.

"Or you could just stay in, and come into my bed later tonight," he proposes, playing with a lock of my hair.

I'm torn. While that sounds fun, I was also looking forward to letting loose tonight. Not as much as I have, but I've been working hard and deserve a little celebration.

"Or you could come out. And stay in my bed," I tease again, drawing a finger up and down his chest.

Mick tilts his head to the side, screwing his mouth up.

"Nahhh, I think I'm going to stay in. But have fun. Maybe we can keep things *casual* another night this weekend."

Just like I did to him, he's laying some ground rules. He's not going to adjust his life to fit mine, like so many guys would and have, and I'm going to have to swallow that bitter pill.

We leave the bathroom separately, and Madison and Christine didn't even notice I was gone for longer than usual.

20

The email came in a day ago, while I was researching a project for my Molecular Control of Metabolism and Metabolic Disease course.

At first, I thought it was a prank because part of me never actually thought I'd hear back from him. But when Dr. Francis Richards asks you to come to his office during his open hours, you go. Even if you think it's another one of your classmates messing with you.

Even though the door is open, I still knock, and he turns from his desk.

"Ah, Mr. Barrett, I've been expecting you. Come in, take a seat."

I do as I'm told. "Hello, Dr. Richards, thank you for calling me in."

My hands are a little sweaty, and I'm glad he's not holding out a hand for me to shake. His office is beige with little to no personal accents, aside from a wedding picture set next to the computer monitor on the desk.

"Let's get right to it. You came up with these theories?" he asks, tossing my notebook onto the table.

I can't tell from his voice whether he's pissed off, impressed, or a little bit of both. "Yes, sir."

"And how did you come to these conclusions, or well, schools of thought? They're not fully formed, testable approaches." He's schooling me on how things are done, and that's fine.

He thinks I'm trying to be a smart-ass, by giving my notebook to him, but all I want is to pick his brain and learn everything there is to know from him.

"I was the sole caretaker for my dad for about three of the six years since he was diagnosed with ALS. I've observed his behavior, accompanied him on every gym or physical therapy session, have recorded his daily routines, and studied his lab and blood results from numerous tests over the years. I know I'm only scratching the surface, and my theories may be way off, but I believe some of the things in that notebook could help patients in the long run."

It's cocky, talking to the foremost expert on ALS research as if I, some junior nobody, could give him the next major breakthrough. But I have to be. Not because I'm so confident in myself, but because my confidence in my research could help save my father's life.

He nods slowly, assessing me. This is not a hurried man, even from the first five seconds of meeting him, you can tell, Dr. Richards doesn't hastily make any decision.

He pushes a finger into the cover of the notebook. "I've explored some of these very minimally, but I have to say, not even my fourth-year fellows are thinking like this. Color me impressed, Mr. Barrett. As you might know, I get a ton of interest in my trials and research, and most of the time, the people who think they can contribute are very far off the mark. But some of your insights, well, they had my mind working. Which not a lot of people can accomplish."

Honestly, I'm floored. It's as close to a compliment that a

world-renowned doctor will ever give you, and I'm practically a pool of giddy science geek excitement at my shoes.

"Thank you. I ... thank you for simply reading through it," I say, nodding and trying to keep my composure.

"Now, I told you I don't do this, and I don't. I usually go through the proper application process, and I never accept undergrads. But you said you'd be willing to do whatever it took, and I think you might be valuable on an upcoming trial I'm trying to propose."

"Absolutely. I'll help in whatever way you need." Now I'm sitting on the edge of my seat, not only not keeping my cool but looking like a total lap dog.

Dr. Richards holds his hands up. "It's going to be a lot of late nights and early mornings. A lot of coffee runs and menial tasks. The most advanced thing you'll probably do is input data. You won't be able to provide feedback or discuss with the other fellows or medical students. On top of your course load, this will be a lot. And we'll expect you to do it with no objections and no complaints. Is that clear?"

I don't even blink at his red flags. "Yes, of course. I'm prepared to help in whatever way I can."

Because even if I can't give input, I can sit in the room with these minds. While breakthroughs are made, while they teach me so much more than I'd ever learn on my own, in a classroom, or probably for another several years.

"And I know you have a personal bias where ALS is concerned. That's both your biggest weakness and strongest motivator. It's healthy to have a passion for the medicine you're working on. It's not when it becomes an obsession, when you put all else aside to get to an answer we may be years away from. I want you to remember that."

The reality of that is harsh, but necessary.

"I expect you tomorrow morning, at six a.m. You'll work on

the data logs from tonight's lab session with my medical students, and I'd like a dry cappuccino. And while you're here tomorrow, photocopy your notebook for me and leave the sheets on my desk."

Dr. Richards doesn't say goodbye, and I don't linger. He's a man with limited time, and I just took up some of the precious seconds.

I wait until I'm outside of the medical building to pump my fist in victory, because I just did what other undergrads only dream of doing.

It doesn't even bother me that I'll have to drag myself out of bed tomorrow morning, I'm that excited.

21

JOLIE

W e're almost at midterms, and I've managed to keep my secret from everyone except for Mick.

My best friends are none the wiser to the wool being pulled over their eyes, and no one has yet to recognize me on the Salem Community College campus. Or witness me sneaking back on Salem Walsh. I have had to get crafty a couple of times, having Mick swipe me into the library and actually having to leave the Pub once because their regular credit card machine was broken again. But other than that, I've been extremely lucky.

It's a godsend I wasn't living in the dorms when all of this happened, because I would have had to move out, and that would have been tricky to explain.

I'm not just keeping this secret for pride anymore, either. I'm doing surprisingly well in my classes and carrying a 3.8 GPA for the semester. Biology is my toughest course, but with Mick's help, I've been surviving enough to earn my A.

Not that we've only been studying. Since the day in the Rowan's bathroom, we've seen each other three times. Not the night of the party, no, he held strong even when I drunk texted him at two a.m. to come over. He hadn't even answered, and I'd heard from him the next morning to let me know he'd been asleep. But the day after that, we'd had a nighttime study session that ended with sex in his car. And then the next day, he'd come over while my roommates were at class. Finally, the Tuesday after that, we studied in the biology lab after hours, and may or may not have fucked in the utility closet close by.

No matter how mature both of us said we were trying to be, we can't seem to stop sneaking into places one should never have sex in. When we're studying, I find myself admiring the tautness of his jaw, or his hand wanders over to plant itself on my thigh.

So far, he seems fine with keeping us casual, *and* keeping my secret. He's the most trustworthy person I've ever met in my life, and it's a wonder more people aren't like him. I think it's because he grew up in a household where lying and manipulating weren't in your parent's job descriptions.

Well, Mick and Jennifer, are keeping my secret. I suspect that she suspects something is up, because of how I'm always lurking around and bolting for the door after classes are through. We actually have three of our five together, weirdly enough, and we've become buddies.

Today, she's saved me my usual seat as I hightail it into Business Ethics.

"Almost missed that check in. Did you bring them?" Her violet hair is twisted up in a knot on her head today.

Throwing myself into the chair beside her, I pull out my clicker. It's a device that allows students to check themselves into a class, since some college professors still like to count attendance toward a grade. I check myself in, and I must have thirty seconds left, because the professor starts talking at that very moment.

We're seated in the back of the lecture hall, so I talk to

Jennifer in a hushed voice, ignoring whatever is going on down below. This class is so easy, I don't even need to study for it. Determining what is right and wrong? Yeah, I've gotten a few lessons on that already.

"If *someone* hadn't made me stop for burritos, I wouldn't have almost missed my window to sign in." I scowl at her, pulling a cylinder wrapped in foil out of my bag.

"Not my fault you ran late. I bought lunch last time, and you pass the best burrito place on your way." She rubs her hands together before accepting the burrito and unwrapping it.

No one pays us any mind, because they're all probably working on other homework in the stadium seating in front of us. Or, more likely, they're playing Internet games or sexting on their phones.

"Did you get queso?" she asks.

"It's going to get messy," I argue.

We eat lunch together every day in this class, since it's boring and I'm always running from one place to another. We never actually get a chance to sit down and talk, so we use Business Ethics as our gossip time.

"Who cares?" Jennifer rolls her eyes, and I hand it over.

We unwrap our burritos as quietly as we can and then begin eating. I find it hilarious that this professor wants to take attendance, but then doesn't seem to even notice that his entire class isn't paying attention to his lecture. We're literally acting like Carrie Bradshaw and her friends, lunching in the park, and he's worried about if I'm sitting in my seat.

"So, how was your concert?" I ask.

Jennifer told me a few weeks ago that she's a promoter for a couple of nightclubs in the area. I think it's pretty cool, and it definitely suits her. She's given me a couple of bands to listen to, and while they're not completely my thing, I like a few songs.

"Insane. The place was packed, like four hundred people, and I almost got punched in the face in the mosh pit."

This girl knows designer labels, dances in mosh pits, and can eat ghost peppers like they're gummy bears. Seriously, she asked me to get extra jalapeños on her burrito.

I cringe. "Sounds painful."

She chuckles. "I would love to see you out there. You should come to my next event."

I shrug, because it could be fun. I'm always the type of person to try something once. "Yeah, maybe."

"What's going on over in your secret world? Does anyone know you come here yet?"

See, I knew she knew something was up. She's hinted at it before, but now she's straight up asking.

"This ... one guy does." My eyes dart around.

She lifts an eyebrow. "Oh?"

It seems she's more intrigued about the guy than my secret, but I can't really explain one without the other.

I sigh, biting into my chicken and guacamole-filled tortilla. "Don't tell anyone this, okay? But I'm a student at Salem Walsh. Or ... I was. I got in trouble last year, and this is my punishment. If I make good grades this year, I get to re-enroll for my senior year."

"What did you do?" she immediately asks.

There was no surprise in her eyes when I told her my biggest secret, and Jennifer is way smarter than anyone, especially me, enrolled at this community college. It pisses me off that she can't go to a four-year, or that her parents won't let her stop going to school and turn to promoting. She revealed to me that her biggest dream would be to manage a road team for a band and travel all over the world. I told her she should do it, that I've been backstage and seen the intricate setups those tours have. But she said her parents would pull what little funding they do give her to live, and so she's shit out of luck until she can save up more money.

I weigh telling her. "It's not important, anyway—"

"What did you do?" she presses, wiping a dab of queso off the corner of her mouth.

I roll my eyes, bracing myself internally. "I skinny-dipped in one of the famous fountains on campus and spray-painted the junk of the statues in the fountain."

Jennifer's eyes dance with amusement as she slaps a hand over her mouth. She starts choking on her laughter, and a few people turn around. I snap forward, facing the front of the classroom and hoping to God the professor doesn't look up here. When Jennifer stops choking, I finally turn back to her.

"You happy now?"

She breathes and wipes her eyes. "You have no idea. So, the guy. Go on."

"He's the only one there who knows. But, we met before this semester started, at a summer camp we were both working at."

She looks up wistfully. "Ah, summer lovin', had you blast?"

I chuckle. "Yes, and it did happen so fast."

"Did he get friendly down in the sand?"

This bit is getting old, but is making me giggle so I continue it for a final time. "We definitely made out under the dock."

"Okay, enough." She slices a hand through the air. "So, you're dating him now?"

"Not exactly. I'd call it ... friends with benefits, maybe? Or a casual hookup buddy? He's tutoring me for biology, and he's so freaking smart. Not my usual type."

"That could be a good thing. I feel like your usual type are the ones who get you to spray-paint classical statues in the nude."

She's not wrong. "Yeah, I've never really had a long-term

thing, though. I've had boyfriends, but they've all fizzled out. Nothing serious. With him ... it just feels different."

Jennifer takes a few bites and seems to be thinking to herself. "Did I tell you I almost got married?"

"What?" I nearly shout, because it's so surprising.

No one turns around though, and Professor Oblivious is still dithering on up front.

She nods. "I was with my high school boyfriend for four and a half years. When we turned twenty, we were going to elope. Thought love could conquer all, told anyone who disagreed to fuck off."

"So, did you?" I ask.

Jennifer shakes her head, popping the rest of her burrito in her mouth. "No. Every time I tried to envision wearing his ring or what our life would look like even a year down the line, all of these things kept popping up. Little habits of his that annoyed me, or big things, like his lack of ambition. I might not be a scholar, but I hustle for my passion. Over time, he stopped being interested in what I said when I spoke, and I knew it would only get worse. I called it off four days before we were set to road trip to Vegas."

Wow. I look at her in a completely different light now. It's funny, how you think you know someone. I tout myself as a person who can get a pretty good handle on another person within a few minutes of meeting and talking to them. But I've been proved so wrong in the last couple of months. First with Mick, and now Jennifer.

There are so many layers to people, ones they never show you unless they trust you enough to be vulnerable.

"Do you regret it? Was he mad?"

"He was pretty upset, but I don't regret it. He went on to start dealing drugs in our town, got caught with a pretty big load of cocaine and is in jail for a year or two. But besides that, because obviously I didn't know that was going to happen when I broke it off, I just ... we weren't going to love each other forever, you know? I could tell that. I think that when you know it's not right, you just know. A lot of people like to say that they don't know if this person is *the one* or if that person is the one, but you know. And even if they don't have to be the one, you know when a guy is worth more than just a few romps in the sack."

Her words ring true, right to my gut. I've known since the second week of summer that there was something different about Mick, but I refused to acknowledge it. Now that our situation could be more permanent, I was still trying to throw curveballs in my way. We both have our separate problems and goals, I know that. But if we're spending so much time together anyway, there's no reason we couldn't ... commit. Right?

Jesus, did I just give myself permission to commit?

Maybe I am taking this whole maturity thing to the next level.

I think this is as I pour some chipotle ranch dressing onto my burrito, in the back of a lecture hall, as I ignore the professor who is teaching.

22

"If you keep doing that, I'm going to come."

Mick's face is screwed up in concentration, his hands locked on my hips.

I'm bent over him, my hands on the tufted headboard of my bed, as I rise up and slowly wiggle back down.

"But it feels too good." I sigh as I sink fully down onto him. "I thought you could go all night."

He smacks my ass lightly. "No one's saying I can't. But when you suck my dick within an inch of its life, it doesn't leave much hope for me holding out."

I repeat the motion over, relishing the hot-cold tingles that shoot down my spine.

"God, you're so sexy." He brushes a hand over my collarbone, and it finds its way down to my breast.

He plucks at my nipple as I ride him, short, moaning breaths releasing from my throat. I get lost in the moment, throwing my head back as I grind down onto him and then pull back up. Each time I do, it hits my G-spot, something I've never found with anyone other than Mick.

As if he knows I need a little more to get there, he wraps a fist around my loose locks, pulling on them. The small bite of pain in my scalp spurs me on, and with Mick's fingers rolling my nipple, I give in.

"Come on, Jolie, let me feel you." He groans.

The orgasm washes over me, and I know I'm being loud as it ravages my senses, but I don't care.

At the last second, Mick flips me over, coming down on top of me as he pounds with full force. The move makes my orgasm last, waves still crashing as he grunts his release into my shoulder.

After a few beats, he rolls to his back again, taking me with him. I'm tucked into his side, a smile spreading on my face.

We lie in my bed, sated, and idly I think that there is no way Christine and Madison didn't just hear that. They're both home, and Mick and I have been getting more careless. We see each other at least four times a week, which feels way more than casual, and we haven't even been bothering to hook up while my roommates aren't home.

The discussion I had with Jennifer the other day plays in my head, about commitment and following my gut when I know it's the right thing. But I'm too chicken right now. Both Mick and I have skirted around the issue and turned each other down. We finally seem to be in a good spot, why ruin this?

"Are you nervous about midterms?" I ask, playing with the smattering of hair on his pecs.

He gives a tiny shrug. "Some of my classes are more difficult than others, but I'm not too worried."

I snort. "You're literally taking classes that sound like they're seminars out of NASA, and you're going to have a four point oh at the end of this term, I just know it."

Mick runs a hand up and down my bare back. "It's just one of my strengths. Trust me, everyone has their weaknesses."

I wonder absently if he's talking about me. Not only have we not talked about commitment, but we haven't spoken about the truce we broke. We both said it would be better to be friends. He claimed he had too much going on, and I promised him not to pursue anything further. We'd both failed and had yet to acknowledge that.

"How about you, how are you feeling about midterms?" He tucks a lock of hair behind my ear.

I shrug. "Okay, I guess. I feel like I've been studying my ass off, but unfortunately, school just isn't as easy for me as it is for you. I get into those exams sometimes and just freeze up, or my mind goes blank. Or I just end up putting down the wrong answers, even if I think they're right. I'm freaking out about it a little."

Mick tips my chin up from where I was sulking on his chest. "Hey now, none of that. You have been working so hard, and I know you're going to do well. You're much smarter than you give yourself credit for, Jolie."

The words are sincere, and it's the first time I think anyone has ever called me smart. Why does this guy have to be here at this time, when neither of those two things seem to match up to my plan right now? I don't think I'm ready to knowingly step into something serious, because I've got a lot on the line with school.

Does the universe know that? Did it drop Mick in my path to test me, or to help me out?

"Thanks." I clear my throat, uncomfortable with the compliment. "Are you going home for Thanksgiving break?"

Now Mick's face becomes clouded with something I can't read, and I know I've hit on those skeletons in his closet.

"Yeah, but only for a few days. I have to be back on campus for this thing I'm doing."

I don't bother asking about his parents, as he's revealed little about them, even when we were at camp this summer.

"What's that? Is this the mysterious job you're always saying you can't stay over for?" He's left my house late at night or we've parted ways after studying because he has to be up early most mornings.

He begins kneading his knuckles into my shoulder, and holy crap does it feel amazing. "It's actually this clinical trial I'm helping with in the medical school. Well, I wouldn't say helping. I'm basically a runt intern, but they're doing a lot of research over Thanksgiving break and want me back here."

I sit up on an elbow, leaning into his chest. "Wait a minute, you're an intern on a medical trial?"

"Yeah." He blinks at me.

"That's like really advanced, isn't it? I mean, I know very little about medical trials, but don't you have to be a doctor or something?" My mind is blown.

Mick chuckles. "Or a doctor in training. I basically begged my way in and get them coffee. Don't be impressed."

My mouth forms an O. "Of course I'm impressed! Jeez, you're way too intelligent for me."

He laces his fingers in mine. "Don't say that."

But it's true. Mick is so impressive, light-years ahead of me in so many ways, and it's kind of intimidating.

"You're so impressive. Someday, I'll get to call you Dr. Barrett. That's pretty sexy. Can I come to you for a checkup?" I flirt with him, walking my fingers up his chest.

It's easier this way, when we don't have to talk about serious things. Talking about that can lead to discussing other things, like what we're doing or where it's going.

There is a devilish gleam in his eye. "I think I can give you a checkup right now."

I've just finished my sixth episode of *Game of Thrones*, and the Pepsi on my nightstand is almost empty when my phone buzzes.

Jolie: *Drunk. Mish you.*

Well, someone is clearly having a good time. When she told me she was going out tonight, I told her of my plans and she'd booed me. I know she would have liked to tote me around like a puppy dog, grinding against her on some dirty living room dance floor, but it's not my scene.

Her misspelling makes me smile. The only time I've ever seen Jolie truly drunk, she was a total mess. But she's said she's taking it easier, and I believe her if she can send texts with just one slip up.

Mick: *What're you doing over there, party girl?*
Jolie: *Horny. Want uuuuu*
Mick: *Oh yeah? Well, I'm already in bed.*

While her drunk texting always makes me laugh, I haven't given in yet. She's reached out on about four occasions, wanting me to meet her back at her house after her night of partying. Actually, she always invites me out, which I guess is better than getting a booty call at the end of the night. But I didn't want to be that person, showing up to a girl's house just because she asked me to come crawling.

My feelings for Jolie are already complicated as it is. We said we're keeping things casual, but aside from courses and my internship, I barely think of anything else but her. I'd missed two phone calls from Mom this week while Jolie and I were "studying." One of my assignments was turned in twenty minutes late because I'd forgotten after an hour in Jolie's bed.

This isn't casual, even though the two of us refuse to acknowledge that it isn't. And it's making me mess up the very things I told her I wouldn't dare allow to be messed up. My future, my dreams of being a doctor, and everything I'm working toward to help my Dad and his disease ... I wasn't making them a priority.

But part of me can't stop. The more time I spend with her, the more I realize that not everything in life depends on science and logic. When I'm around Jolie, I find my heart doing a backflip every time she smiles. I find my pulse quickening when she leans into me, or my breath catching when she touches me ever so slightly.

These aren't explainable bodily reactions, and yet, most people would call them ... love.

My phone vibrates again before I can get anymore in my own head.

Jolie: *Boring! Don't you want sex?*

I weigh that in my mind. Of course, I want sex, but I'm not going to be the one who always goes to her. Thus far, I've gone to her off-campus house. I've met her at the times she can and implicitly agreed to leave her house in a hurry so that her roommates don't see me. But I also want to see her ... desperately. So I try a new tactic.

Mick: *You can come over here if you can get a safe ride.*

On the one hand, I'm not sure how drunk she is, or how drunk whoever she's with is. Maybe I should have offered to drive down and pick her up, but that would defeat the purpose of having her come to me. It's a test, to see if this really is casual, or if we need to have a larger conversation.

Jolie: *What's ur dorm and room? I'm comin.*

Well, I guess that settles that. I text out the answer and then drop the phone on the bed. My fingers drum on my stomach, and I'm both impatient and anxious. I've never told a girl to come to me. It feels out of my nature, and the pit in my stomach is there because I'm not sure how to do this whole "college booty call thing." Not that this is that, but it's the first time I've had someone over late night.

And well, I'm a newb when it comes to having any sort of game.

Twenty minutes later, Jolie texts that she's coming up in the elevator. I pass two of my roommates in the living room, and it occurs to me that maybe I should have given them a courtesy heads up that I was having a girl over. But they've never given me that, and I haven't minded, so here we are.

Paul and Rodney are in the living room, playing video games, when I go out to get the door.

"Hi gorgeous." Jolie leans into me, snuggling herself into my chest.

My arms come around her, and behind me, I hear two loud thumps. Turning, both Jolie and I see the two guys staring at us, eyes as wide as saucers.

"Hey." Jolie wags her fingers at them. Her breath smells like cinnamon, and she sways on her feet a little. "I'm Jolie."

A beat of silence passes, and then Paul jumps out of his chair. "Uh ... I'm Paul. Welcome, I'm Paul."

Yep, he introduces himself. Twice. In the same sentence. That makes Jolie giggle, and Rodney can do little more than offer a wave.

"We're just going to go back to my room, okay?" I tell them, taking Jolie by the hand.

I don't feel like making a spectacle right now, and it's late.

"We're talking about this later!" Rodney calls down the hall, and Jolie giggles.

"Mmm, I missed you." She loops her arms around my neck, her soft skin surrounding me.

I walk us backward into my room, nuzzling in her neck. Instantly, my cock is hard. "Missed you, too."

I'm not sure, but I don't think friends with benefits or booty calls say that type of thing to each other.

My mouth meets hers, and before long, we're making out in the middle of my tiny dorm room. Jolie cups me over my sweatpants, and I grind into her palm. Just as I'm about to start undressing her, her stomach gives a loud whine.

We break apart, laughing, as she presses a hand to her abdomen. "Ugh, seems like I have the drunk munchies. Got any snacks around here?"

"So you come over here to steal my food?" I tease her, palming her cheek in my hand.

"Feed me, Seymour!" She does the voice of the Audrey II

from *Little Shop of Horrors*, and I might have just fallen head over heels.

"All right, let me see what I can scrounge up." Though it means going to face the firing squad my roommates surely have planned.

I'm not wrong, because as I pull a bag of microwaveable popcorn out of the cabinet, Paul and Rodney corner me.

"Um, dude, that's Jolie Kenner." Rodney slaps my arm.

"Ouch." I rub at the spot. "I know that."

"Don't play smart, dumbass! How did we not know that you were boning Jolie Kenner?" Paul practically screeches.

I roll my eyes, because they're being douches. "I'm not boning anyone. Jolie and I ... we met before I came to Salem Walsh. I like her. That's all you need to know."

Rodney throws his hands up. "This dude is hooking up with the hottest girl on campus, and he doesn't even think it's a big deal."

"Maybe it's because I look at her as a person, not a campus celebrity. She's a great girl, and you better treat her with respect. I don't want to hear any of that boning crap, got it?" I point my finger in their directions.

Something in my blood is boiling, because they're treating her like some kind of superstar instead of the genuinely funny, nice female I've come to know. I have a feeling a lot of people regard Jolie that way, which is why she's so quick to bottle herself up, or take on the party girl persona they expect of her.

"Got it." Rodney nods. "Sorry, man. We didn't mean anything by it. Just a little shocked."

Paul nods along with his friend. "Yeah, sorry, man. Didn't mean any offense."

By the time I make it back to my room with her popcorn and water, she's asleep on the bed. She's curled up on my pillow, her dress riding up her thighs, and her heels are still on. Carefully, as not to wake her, I unlace the intricate straps from her ankles and place them on the floor. I help unzip her, and she mumbles a bit as I get her out of the silky pink slip of a dress, but doesn't wake. For a split second, I wonder if this is creepy; me undressing her. But I figure she's safer like this, and wouldn't mind if I got her naked to snuggle. I mean, that's what she came over here for in the first place.

Once she's undressed, I shuck everything but my boxers and climb onto the bed, pulling the covers over us both as I snuggle her gently against my chest.

It's the first time we've strictly slept together, much less in a bed. It's also the first time we've been intimate without having sex. And for me, it's the first time I've ever had a girl in my bed to stay the night.

I know she might not remember it in the morning, but I relish the moment, breathing her in. The dark swathes us, and I can practically feel my heart crack wide open, emotion for her pouring out in my joints and tendons.

She's invaded me, and I know now that I won't be able to detach from her.

Not that I even want to.

24

My eyes blink against the dim light of the room, the angle coming from the window different than where my bed is in my off-campus house.

It takes me a minute to remember where I am, but when a sleeping Mick shifts against my back, it comes back to me. I came to his dorm last night.

Honestly, my head isn't hazy and I do remember everything I did last night, which means I controlled my drinking. Of that I'm proud. But I don't remember getting undressed, or under the covers with him, so I must have passed out here.

Dammit. My first sleepover with Mick and I don't even have the memories to obsess over when I'm alone. Rolling over, I snuggle into his arms, trying to soak up the last moments of our sleepover.

I've slept in guys beds, even had some long-term flings that turned into a weeknight stay over situation. But I never cared about those guys like I do with Mick. It's the first time he's invited me over, and even if we are smooshed in a twin bed, my skin is tingling with the closeness and my heart is beating double time.

I try to sneak a peek around his room, but it's mostly empty. There are a few photos I can't make out over on his desk, which is piled high with books and papers. The open closet seems neat enough, with shirts on hangers and a few jackets or sweatshirts near the right side. There is no mess on the floor, but I wouldn't expect there to be, and it smells nice enough. His sheets are a navy blue, with a matching plaid comforter.

Mick's fingers start to stroke slowly up and down my back, eliciting goose bumps.

"Mmm, feels good," I whisper, trying to nuzzle in as close as possible.

He doesn't say anything, just kisses my temple as he continues slowly scratching my back. I could get used to this, waking up beside him. The thought both makes my heart drop to my knees, and calms it. Because I'm very in tune with how I feel about this guy, but it scares the crap out of me. I've never wanted more than a few nights of fun, but with him, I'd rather the mornings after and the in-betweens than the sexy times.

Which is a big feeling to swallow.

"Morning." His deep, sleep-coated voice meets my ear.

"Morning." I smile, pulling back to look at him.

I don't even feel self-conscious, with the need to brush my teeth or go dab some eye cream on my bags, because I'm too busy studying him. If it's possible, Mick is more handsome when he's just woken up. His thick, straight hair is tossed this way and that, with those moss green eyes full of drowsy dreams. His skin is warm against my touch, and with the way he's looking at me, I know what's on his mind.

"You have fun last night, party girl?" he teases me in a quiet voice.

Then I fully remember why I went out last night. Not only had I passed my biology midterms, but I'd gotten good grades in all of my other courses as well.

"Today is the last day of this half of the semester," I say, suddenly sitting upright.

"Yeah?" Mick turns into me, cuddling against my side.

Looking down at him, I brush his burnt auburn hair off his forehead. "I usually take myself to the beach today, walk in the water, and maybe grab lunch. It's the last nice day of the season, typically, and it's tradition. Would you want to come?"

It's a big thing, me inviting him to my beach day. I've done it since freshman year, before Christine and Madison were my true friends. I needed to get away, to be alone before I went home to the frigidity of life with my parents. I usually do this more than once a year, and find places off the beaten path like the seafood hut I took Mick to before, but this end of midterm beach day is an annual thing.

"Sure." He looks at me, and I can tell that he knows this is more than an invitation to walk on the sand.

With the sheet falling away from me, I see that I'm naked. "Did you undress me last night?"

Mick shrugs. "When you fell asleep on my pillow like some kind of cat who'd claimed her territory, I figured I'd take your heels off. Might fall on your way to a late night bathroom trip. And then I figured it would only make you more comfortable if you weren't wearing that dress."

I roll my eyes, because it's such a guy answer. "Well, you better get me a big T-shirt, because I'm not wearing that thing home. And we're stopping off at my place on the way."

Thirty minutes later, and we're sitting in the front seat of his car, on the way to the beach. I changed into a pair of jean shorts and a light sweater, with the weather turning as it is. After that, I grab two of the beach chairs I keep stocked, and a small cooler with waters and lemonade. I never drink on this outing, it's kind of a sacred thing.

"So you do this every year?" Mick asks, following the GPS on his phone that's mounted on the dashboard.

I nod. "Yep. I started freshman year. I was in a weird phase, not really feeling a part of anywhere. I didn't live at home anymore, and the dorm didn't feel like the place I belonged either. I was questioning some of the friendships I'd made, and then I read something that being near water helped to center you, so I decided to give it a try. It actually worked, so I come back often, but this trip I do alone right before I go home to ..."

I trail off, not really knowing how to describe my parents.

"You don't really talk about them a lot," Mick says, acknowledging that I was about to say something about my home life.

"You don't either," I counter, being defensive.

His jaw tics. "You're right. But you told me you'd be there for me if I ever needed it, and I want to be able to give you the same. You can talk to me."

Those strong hands and serious eyes stay trained on getting us to our destination, but I know he's listening.

I shrug, not knowing where to start. I've never expressed any of this to anyone.

"I guess it makes me sound like a spoiled brat, because I've never really wanted for anything, but I haven't had the best life. Sure, I had money, and *things*. My parents fixed most everything that did go wrong, up until last year with this suspension. But I've never really had anyone *care* about me. They were always too busy with work, or their social scene, charities, you name it. They'd bring me along, but we weren't really doing things together. A lot of people would call me ungrateful, but going to different countries and on lavish vacations isn't really fun if no one wants to spend time with you. It's the same when I go home now. We sit down to a meal that none of us helped to cook, don't talk about anything of substance, and then they go off into their own little world."

Mick's hand reaches across the middle console and lands on my thigh. "That doesn't sound spoiled, it sounds neglected. I'm sorry that's how they are."

I shrug. "I've gotten used to it, but it still sucks. Especially when they can't fix a problem. The one thing they've managed to do, protect me when the odds aren't in my favor, is the one thing they failed at this time, which is why I'm in this situation with both schools and my suspension."

"You still never told me what happened with the suspension," he says as he turns into the parking lot I directed him to.

The engine cuts, and then we're just sitting there. It's the most intimate moment I've ever had with another person, and we're not naked or about to do something physical. To me, expressing feelings and emotions is much scarier than getting into bed with someone. This is a real, deep conversation we're having, and Mick has seen a side of me I've never shown anyone else. That's ... heavy.

"I was drunk, with a bunch of my friends you've probably seen me around with. We decided to jump into the fountain, the one in front of the drama building. And ... do it naked. They also brought spray paint cans. My friends happened to hear the campus police sirens, I did not. I got caught, and wouldn't give up the other names. My dad struck a deal with the dean."

It was a simplified version, but now Mick knew more about me than anyone else in my life. I'd kept that story in for so long, that it felt cathartic to let it out.

"So none of your friends came forward?" he asks, anger in his eyes as he turns to me.

I hold my hands up, trying to stop his hate train. "No, they didn't know I even got caught. I didn't tell them. They don't deserve to be sucked into that mess. Remember, they don't even know I'm suspended."

"You sacrificed yourself for your friends. You could have

given them up, taken the easy deal. I'm sure it would have been offered." Mick appears to be chewing this over. "I'd say that's pretty honorable of you."

That makes me blush, and I clear my throat. "Should we go walk a bit?"

Green eyes seem to peer into my soul. "You're a really special person, Jolie. I don't think you've heard that enough, but I'm telling you now."

I blink at him, because he makes me feel like I'm worthy of being with the kind of person he is. "Thanks."

"All right, let's go walk. Maybe I'll throw you in the ocean." His smile taunts me as he moves to get out of the car.

For two years, I've been coming to this spot alone, a part of the beach with a neat cove you can explore. It's on the end of the island located near campus, and there isn't much but a couple of gorgeous houses down this way.

Mick and I walk for an hour, maybe more, up and down the sand, talking and flirting and splashing each other.

I thought I would always walk this spot alone, but I found out today that walking it hand in hand with someone who is quickly becoming my everything ... well, that's even better.

25

Thanksgiving break is a blur, with a visit home doing nothing to calm my nerves.

I manage to get into three fights with Mom in the four days I'm home. They're all over Dad's care and what I don't think she's doing right. I make her cry on more than one occasion, and Dad gets so angry that his blood pressure sky rockets and I have to have one of his doctor's call in a new prescription on the morning of Thanksgiving.

I don't mean to be an asshole, but giving up the reins after being his full caretaker for almost three years is difficult. And with all I'm learning in Dr. Richards' lab, I feel like I can implement so many new things to give him a better quality of life.

Overall, the day of Thanksgiving is nice. We all cook together, well, Mom and I cook while Dad sits in his wheelchair watching us. I tell them about school, and the internship. I watch some football with Dad, because I know he loves it, even though I can't stand sports.

But the next day, I had to go back to campus. The research stage of the trial, before it even started, was getting intense, and Dr. Richards needed all hands on deck.

Something about being home, about taking on such a heavy load of schoolwork and internship and everything else that was going on in my life ... it was getting to me.

Not to mention I haven't seen Jolie in a week. I hate to admit that it's one of the things putting me most on edge, but it is. We've texted every day, and talked on the phone once or twice, but it isn't the same. The woman is becoming my addiction, as unrealistic as that is. I'm a scientist, a simply left-brained individual who, before, never believed in all that "love cures all" or "feeling with your heart" mentality.

But I haven't felt her against me in too long, and I'm starting to go insane because of it.

It's a good thing she's coming to this benefit dinner tonight ... though maybe it's not because it'll be a solid couple of hours where I can't put my hands on her.

Dr. Richards insisted that all the interns working on the ALS clinical trial be in attendance for this benefit auction dinner and said we could bring a date. The dinner is more like a gala where rich donors for the university and the medical school come to hob knob while throwing money at us to fund our trial. The medical school's auditorium has been transformed into a black and silver ball sort of thing, with ribbons and fancy tablecloths everywhere. There is a quartet playing in the corner, and the auction tables are on the back wall.

I peruse them as I wait for Jolie, and I'm honestly stunned that people can even afford to own stuff like this in the first place, much less auction some of the experiences off. One week at this couple's home in Aspen, another weekend at a private estate in Martha's Vineyard. Tickets to Broadway shows, courtside seats to a Bobcats game, and a wine tour of Italy for two weeks. I think I even see a private yacht experience down the row.

Yeah, I can't afford any of that. But if rich people are going to spend their money to fund a cause that might somewhere down the line cure my dad's disease? I'm all for it.

I'd never asked someone to accompany me to something. Hell, I hadn't even asked someone to my senior prom. I wasn't sure how to go about it, so one night over break I'd called Jolie and just asked her. She seemed flattered and smitten, in a way only girls can seem when you ask them out somewhere fancy.

My next problem was securing a suit nice enough for the event. Mom had pulled out one of Dad's old suits, and it fit well enough, though I probably looked like a chump compared to the people attending this benefit.

The doors to the auditorium open, and a bunch more people spill in. There must be at least two hundred people here so far, and more keep coming.

A flash of deep purple catches my attention, the crowd parts, and there she is.

Jolie, standing there in that dress, knocks the air out of my lungs.

She walks down the aisle, her mocha waves fluttering over her shoulder as she turns her head this way and that, looking for me. All of those locks look like molten chocolate, flowing down her back and around her shoulders. The deep purple, almost black gown looks velvet and hugs every curve of her perfect body. Her eyes are rimmed with dark makeup, and the effect only makes her look even more like some kind of earth angel among us ordinary specimens.

When she catches my eye, she smiles, her mauve lips full and painted. My cock twitches at the thought of smearing it off.

My heart gallops double-time, and my hands both sweat with anxious energy and itch to touch her.

"Thank you for coming. You look ... holy crap." I can't stop looking at her.

Jolie's cheeks flush a shade of pink, and she chuckles. "I think that's the first time I've heard you curse."

"That outfit, you ... it's deserved."

"I'm just glad you asked me. I don't like not seeing you, and you clean up pretty well." She moves into me, pressing up on her toes to give me a kiss on the cheek.

It's been seven days since we touched each other, since we laid eyes on each other, and I suddenly wish I hadn't seen her here first. The strongest urge to pull her into a dark corner and kiss her senseless comes over me, and I know I need to get it under control. This is an important night for the trial, and I want to represent Dr. Richards well.

"I missed you, too." I breathe into her hair and then kiss the top of her head.

Those words, and the gesture, are more intimate than just a casual girl on my arm at a benefit gala.

On the quiet nights at home, where my parents slept in the room a door over and my college roommates weren't screaming at their video games in our dorm room, I thought about her. I thought about how serious things had become, how each time I was with her, it was getting harder and harder to hold that four-letter word on my tongue. I'm falling in love with Jolie, in such a natural way that it scares me. So clearly, I can see how she would fit into my life. When I have a bad day, she's the one I want to lean on, and when I pass a test or get great feedback from Dr. Richards, she's the one I want to tell.

"This is so cool. And this is all for the trial?" Jolie asks, looping her arm in mine.

"Yeah, they have some pretty swanky auction items and trips over there. Want to open your checkbook?" I wink at her.

She gives me a devilish smile. "You know, my parents were a pain in the ass over break. Dropping a couple thousand of their money for a good cause might make me feel better."

Jolie had texted me nonstop about the horrible behavior her parents exhibited over Thanksgiving. They hadn't even bothered to come home for the first three days and claimed they forgot she was going to be home for break. Then, on the fifth day, which was Thanksgiving, they sat down for half an hour, scarfed turkey while looking at their cell phones, and went to a cocktail party that night with friends. Her mom made endless comments about her weight, while her father only spoke to her once and it was to scold her about the trouble she'd gotten in last year. I haven't even met them, and I despise them. They couldn't see the gem they had in front of them, and most of the recklessness or irresponsibleness she exhibited was a direct causation of their lack of love and parenting.

"Win us the yacht trip, that one sounds cool." I wrap my arm tighter around hers, supporting her as she walks.

"Only if you wear a Speedo, real European style." She winks at me.

I crack up. "That would be something, huh? Since we're being European, you're going topless, right?"

Jolie's eyes flash at my forwardness. "I think I like a suited-up Mick. He's very flirty."

My eyes roam over her body. "It's the dress, it's doing things to me."

"Should we blow this popsicle stand?" she suggests.

I look around, spotting Dr. Richards. "I wish we could. Let's at least make it through dinner before I think of unzipping that with my teeth."

"Jesus, Mick." Jolie presses her free hand to her cheeks, the skin there going scarlet.

I think I like being able to take her by surprise.

We check ourselves in at the table where two women sit, directing people to which tables they are to sit at. I give my name, and they confirm our attendance and then give us two tickets for the bar, and our table number. When we make it to the table, I see it's filled but for our two chairs, and that we're sitting with the rest of the interns on the trial.

"Mick." Jeremy, one of the third-year medical students who is a lead on the trial, nods at me.

"Hi everyone." I nod at them. "This is Jolie."

They introduce their dates, and we all fall into the normal small talk. At first I'm a little concerned. Not only is this not Jolie's type of crowd, but they might not take kindly to her either.

About twenty minutes in, I realize I have nothing to worry about. She's elbow deep in a self-deprecating story about a time she spent in the hospital getting her appendix removed. She tried flirting with a doctor to get her more mint chip ice cream. Little did she know, it was actually the janitor who had come to empty her garbage can, and she was too high on the drugs in her IV to notice.

My fellow interns are enthralled with her, it's written all over their faces. This is one of her best attributes; her ability to play to a crowd. She holds court over any room she's in, and it complements me. I don't have to do the heavy lifting of small talk, which I hate. Plus, I get to watch her magic at work.

It only serves to make me fall harder for her.

How the hell am I going to keep from telling this girl that I'm in love with her?

"Morning."

Mick kisses my neck, gently moving up and down the column.

I twist into him, giving my muscles a good stretch as he heats up everything south of my waistline.

"Good morning to you." I can't help but press my bare chest farther into his bare chest.

Is it weird that this no longer scares me? That the feeling of waking up next to him gives me butterflies instead of panic-inducing nausea. That I'd prefer a future where we wake up together every day?

I've never felt this way about anyone, and a few weeks ago it would have scared the crap out of me. But the more Mick and I get into this routine, the more of a fixture he is in my day to day, the more I realize that this could be normal for us going forward.

And the more I realize that it's exactly what I want.

If he's not sleeping in my bed, I'm usually in his, despite the one or two nights a week that our schedules don't match up and we can't fall asleep next to each other. What was supposed to be casual, just a good time, has now turned into a relationship. It's just that neither of us are saying it.

It's almost halfway through the second term of the first semester, and Christmas break is only less than a month away. With my own diligence, and Mick's help in the science courses, I'm passing community college with flying colors. He's also, of course, maintaining his 4.0 GPA and is busy as ever with his medical internship. Though I can see the constant worry in his eyes over whatever is going on at home.

A knock sounds at my door, and Mick halts with his hand halfway up my ribcage, headed for my boob.

"Jolie, I made breakfast!"

Christine's voice comes through my door, and I almost forgot her newfound love of Sunday family breakfast. She instated it when we got back from Thanksgiving break, and I have to admit that I like a fresh homemade waffle I didn't have to cook.

But Mick has never been here for one, and he still hasn't met my roommates. I know why I haven't bitten the bullet yet. If I introduce him, if they know he's real, they'll have questions. And that means I have to talk about and openly admit that I'm falling in love with him.

"I'm okay," I yell, trying to make my voice sound tired.

To my surprise, her voice comes through the door, meaning she stayed there to hear my excuse. "Your boyfriend can eat, too. The guy has been screwing you and sneaking out of here for weeks, I think he deserves a pancake." Christine shouts over the sizzle of bacon.

That makes me giggle.

"Feel like breakfast?" I trail a hand up and down Mick's abs.

"Sure." He grins, knowing he's finally gotten his way.

He's been insinuating that he'd like to meet them for weeks.

We both get dressed in our scrubby Sunday clothes and then head out to the kitchen. Mick, per usual, towers over me and makes our ranch feel small. When we walk in, Christine is manning the stove, flipping over what look to be blueberry pancakes, and Maddy is sitting at the kitchen table, head buried in her cell phone.

"Guys, this is Mick." I wave a hand at the tall drink of water behind me.

"Hey there. Thanks for letting me sneak around the past few weeks." He smiles shyly.

Christine looks him up and down, assessing. Madison's head shoots up, and a knowing smile graces her lips.

"Oh, thank you. I haven't heard Jolie make sounds like that —" Madison starts, but I cut her off.

"That's quite enough!" I shout, giving her a stern look.

An awkward silence passes through the kitchen, and I can't tell whether Mick's ears are going to burn off from embarrassment, or if he's going to burst out laughing.

He breaks the quiet. "Can I help with breakfast at all?"

This seems to please Christine, because she gives me a tiny nod of approval. "That's really nice of you, Mick. Neither of these two lazy asses ever offers to help. If you want to make the coffee, we're almost ready here."

Hopping to it, he doesn't even ask how to use our machine. It's a basic pot, but still. I love how in control he is, how nothing ever seems to rattle him.

I grab plates and cutlery, setting the table, all while Madison sits, staring at her phone.

"Um, are you going to help?" I ask.

She sighs, setting her phone down. "It's just this guy from Friday night. I thought we really connected, and he hasn't texted me back at all."

"Who is he?" I ask, because I was at the gala with Mick on Friday.

"Some frat brother who shoved his tongue down her throat

and then offered her molly." I can hear Christine's eye roll from here.

"He did not!" Madison protests. "He was so sweet and offered to walk me home. We talked about our favorite movies, he got me drinks all night. And he was *so* my type."

"But he hasn't texted you back?" I ask, knowing that's not a good sign.

"Maybe he lost his phone, or it's just dead," Madison supplies.

"For two days?" Christine chimes in as she begins to bring plates of heaping breakfast food to the table.

I grimace. "Yeah, sorry, Mads, I don't think that's likely."

"What do you think, Mick? These two are bringing down my mood." She pouts.

Mick looks surprised as he sits down at the end of the table. He didn't bargain being the male view on fuckboys this morning.

"Well, I think that it's probably not likely, but give him a few days. If you hear from him, great. He might be a good one. But if not, move on. You deserve someone really great, with all that Jolie has told me."

I haven't told him much, but he's just being his usual nice, incredible self.

Christine blinks at him, then points a serving fork in his direction. "I like this one. You can keep him."

My eyes connect with Mick's, and my heart feels like it's being shocked by a defibrillator.

I like this one, too, so much so that I *want* to keep him. Possibly forever.

27

I t's only fair that if I got to meet her roommates, she gets to meet mine.

A couple days later, after getting off a phone call with Mom about Dad's impressive progress the past few weeks, Jolie shows up at my dorm room with lunch.

"You said you were too busy for lunch, so I brought it to you." She smiles, holding up a bag that smells suspiciously of brisket tacos.

My mouth waters, and not just over the food. "You didn't have to do that."

She shrugs, bypassing me to come into our suite foyer. It's small, with the tiny kitchen compromised of a hot plate and a mini-fridge next to it.

"I wanted to, plus, then I don't have to be sneaking around campus, pretending to be in classes I'm not actually in."

"Nah, but you literally couldn't even look at a picture. Not one tit." We hear from the living room, which is just feet away.

My three roommates are deep in discussion, and part of me wonders if any of them go to class. They always seem to be home, usually all together.

I'm not sure what they're squabbling about, but Jolie is standing right next to me, so I interrupt them. "Guys, I want you to meet Jolie."

All three heads whip our way, and their eyes are hungry when they look at her. Jealousy boils in my veins, but she reaches out to grab my hand with her free one.

"Nice to meet you!" she says cheerily.

Aside from the night that she showed up to my place drunk, my roommates haven't seen her. We typically spend night's at her house, because who wants to sleep two people in a twin bed? But the times I have brought her here, it's been discreet. I don't like explaining myself to people, and my roommates would only shorten the time I have to spend with her.

"How's it going? I'm Rodney," Rodney finally pipes up, his voice squeaking like a prepubescent teenager.

"Martin." Martin waves.

"Hi, I'm Paul." Paul walks over to shake her hand, which makes her giggle.

"What are you guys doing?" she asks, observing the TV screen.

There is a paused video game on it, something with zombies and a crossbow.

"We were playing this new video game, but then got into an argument. Because Rodney wanted to dip out, and I said it was probably so he could jack it," Paul explains as if this is all matter-of-fact.

Rodney blushes, stammering, "That was *not* the reason."

It probably was the reason, but I wasn't throwing my horse into this argument.

"Anyway, then we got into an argument. Would you rather have to give up video games, or porn?" Martin supplies, filling her in on what they were arguing about.

"Oh my God." I slap a hand to my forehead, because why did he just tell her that.

"Dude!" Rodney slaps our roommate in the bicep.

But next to me, Jolie chuckles. "Hmm ... well, I don't play video games. So, I guess I could give those up, and keep porn. Definitely keeping porn."

And now I'm wondering what kind of porn she watches, what she looks like when she touches herself, and why I've never wondered this before. It would make excellent material for me.

Looking around at the other guys, they're definitely thinking the same thing. Which only makes the green monster inside me rage more.

"That's enough of that." I chuckle, trying to steer her out of the living room.

"I'd give up porn." Paul shrugs. "If I could find it with a real girl, it's better anyway."

"That's kind of romantic." Jolie tips her head to the side, considering the answer.

"Video games, hands down," Rodney offers, even though he was just embarrassed about porn before.

"Same. I could never give up porn." Martin nods vigorously.

How we got on this topic of conversation the moment my ... girl, I guess that's what she is, walked in the door, I'll never know. All I want is some time with her before I have to go back to calling ALS trials around the country to get my Dad into and eat those brisket tacos.

"Which would you give up?" Jolie turns to me.

I really don't want to keep standing here talking about this, but she won't budge her feet to come to my room.

A frustrated breath escapes my throat. "It doesn't really matter to me. I don't care for either, so I don't need to choose."

"What?" Rodney cries. "We knew you didn't like video games, but porn? You don't care for porn?"

"I don't even know what that means," Martin chimes in.

Jolie turns to me. "You don't like either? So you don't watch porn?"

"Are you telling me you don't bop the bologna? Choke the chicken? Fire off some knuckle-children?" Paul asks, incredulous.

I can't even help but crack up at his ridiculous phrasing. "I don't even know where you come up with this stuff. But yes, even though it's highly personal and none of you should be asking, I do ... choke the chicken."

Jolie snorts at my innuendo.

I continue, tapping the side of my temple. "I just don't use porn to do so. I don't need videos, if you catch my drift. I'm a thinker."

They all breathe out a collective *ah*.

"So now that you all know my masturbation preferences, can we eat our lunch now?" I ask her.

Jolie chuckles. "Yes. It was good to meet you guys."

I practically drag her back to my room. Once we're inside, I slam the door closed. "Sorry about them."

"No, I thought it was funny. Although I have so many questions." Jolie presses up on her toes, kissing my cheek, and then flouncing over to sit on my bed.

"Give me a taco, and then maybe I'll answer them," I plead, because I really am hungry.

She opens the bag and lays out the spread on my comforter. I sit beside her, and we clink our tacos together before taking a bite.

"So, you said you don't watch porn. You like to think. Enlighten me on that." Her brown eyes twinkle with amusement, and something purely carnal.

I roll my own. "I've just never been into porn. I tried it, of course, *a lot* when I was first ... *you know*. Discovering myself. But it always came off forced, or creepy. The scenarios are so fake, and I wasn't, I don't know. It didn't do it for me. So I just started thinking of things that would."

"Like what?" She licks a spot of sauce off her pinky finger.

I shrug. "My math teacher in eighth grade, I thought she was cute. Celebrities that interested me. And then when I got some experience, I'd think about those."

Jolie flushes. "That's kind of hot. Do you think about me?"

"Yes, of course. I have since the summer." My cock twitches in my shorts.

I've had so many fantasies of her. She's the main attraction whenever I jerk off now, and probably always will be.

"What do you think about?" She stops eating.

"Your body. The sounds you make. That time we had sex on the obstacle course at camp ..."

Just remembering it makes me so aroused, I'm no longer hungry either. Jolie is looking at me like I'm her next meal, and my dick is begging me to unzipper it and let it out.

A beat of silence passes between us, charged with sexual electricity.

"I think it's time for dessert now." She sets her taco down.

I chuckle. "I have to work, Jolie."

She begins to crawl toward me. "Nothing like a quickie to make your studying more productive."

And with the angle she's stalking me, I can see right down her shirt.

"I think that's a really smart point," I say, right before shoving the food to the floor.

28

JOLIE

The Pub is absolutely packed as my friends slide into our booth.

I beat them here today, having gotten out of my course at the community college early.

"Y'all are going to kill it on Sunday," Darrell tells Charlie.

"You know it. Regional championship, we're going to slaughter them." Andy kisses his own bicep.

I roll my eyes as they all sit with their lunches. "Do we have to do the sports talk today?"

"What would you rather us talk about, periods and pedicures?" Charlie winks at me.

"Yes, because that's what all women talk about." Britta, his girlfriend, hits him gently on the back of the head.

"Damn, you beat the line. It's a madhouse today." Christine points at my sushi tray.

Madison sips what looks like a smoothie. "Everyone is in here before finals, pretending to study. Except they're all doing what we're doing, eating and gossiping."

"Who said we're gossiping?" Darrell asks.

"As if we do anything else. Plus, I have some good juicy stuff.

I heard that the president of that fraternity down the street from us got suspended for trying to wax his roommate's balls during hazing."

"What the fuck is wrong with people?" Britta looks disgusted.

"Yeah, that's messed up. I'd clock a guy if he tried that with me. It's why I stay far away from those houses," Andy says.

And if Andy is saying it, we should all take warning.

I spot a familiar face across the Pub, and without thinking, yell out.

"Mick, hey!" I shout, not thinking of where I am.

He looks up, spotting me at the ten-person booth.

This is the moment we faced almost four months ago, when Mick's appearance in the Pub took me by such surprise that I acted like a total moron. He hesitates, waiting to see if he should come over, and I make up my mind in an instant. My best friends have already met him, we're practically shacking up on the daily, and I'm not the same girl I was months ago.

That's thanks to him. So I wave him over enthusiastically, and I can feel the eyes on me from the table I sit at.

"Hey." He nods at me, and waves to my roommates.

"Come sit with us, do you have lunch yet?" I ask.

It's a big moment, and maybe not everyone at the table understands that, but the two of us do. This was the moment I acted ashamed of him, and it shows how much I care about him, and what we have.

I scoot over, making the tiniest sliver of room on the outside of the booth.

"Yeah, join us," Christine says, smiling.

She's all for our relationship, grilling me each and every day about Mick and when I'm going to lock it down. I don't know what I was so afraid of, keeping the seriousness of our connection from my best friends. They've been nothing but supportive and even complain about when they'll find someone like him for themselves.

Mick heads over, shimmying past other tables packed with students. When he sits down, I can feel how anxious he is.

"This is Mick, he's my ..." I trail off, knowing that I can't call him my boyfriend. "Well, we've been spending lots of time together."

"Oh, I remember *those* early days." Darrell gives me a knowing grin, while his girlfriend Eileen squeezes his arm in recognition.

I duck my head, blushing because this is all so official. "Yes. Anyways, this is the gang."

Everyone goes around and introduces themselves, and I can feel the tension coming off Mick. He's not really a big crowds type of guy. He fakes it when he has to, but mostly he keeps to himself. At the gala he took me to, I did most of the talking, and he seemed to be thankful for that. But these people would have questions, not for me, for him.

Mick is wearing some kind of nerd shirt again, I swear he has a closet full of the geekiest shirts ever, and Charlie notices.

"Dude, you like *Stranger Things*?" Charlie asks, pointing to Mick's shirt.

Mick looks down and then back up. "Yeah, love it. I can't wait for the fourth season to come out."

Charlie leans into the table from the other side. "Aw, man, I *love* that show! I've been getting in heated arguments with Andy about it. So, how can the Mind Flayer be destroyed?"

I have no freaking idea what he's talking about, but apparently Mick does, because he gets so animated when he answers.

"Well, the Mind Flayer's body is dead, but I'm pretty sure the consciousness is still alive and kicking because it latched onto Will. And then we saw that scene with Billy at the pool, so honestly, I'm not sure. Can't wait to see if Eleven can stop him."

"This is all so nerdy, I can't take it," Madison whines.

Andy throws her an annoyed look and goes on to ask Mick some more burning questions on the show. The three of them chatter away, exchanging theories and fandom before telling everyone at the table they need to start watching this show.

I lean over to Christine. "Well, guess I didn't have to worry about him fitting in."

My best friend looks at me and lowers her voice so only I can hear. "This is a good one, Jolie. Don't let him go. I've never seen you as happy and grounded as you have been in the last few months, and Mick is a diamond in this rough, rough sea of men in our generation. You deserve this. He deserves you."

She squeezes my hand under the table and then drops it. I'm floored. It isn't often that Christine praises me, or even stops her analytical, critical brain for enough seconds to appreciate something.

It means a lot that she says that about Mick and me.

It also means that my stubborn mind is in very deep trouble, because my heart has completely fallen for him.

"You really didn't have to come with me."

My hand holds onto Jolie's as we push through the doors of the medical school, our coffees steaming in our other fists. It's early, earlier than I normally go in to do some of the data entry work I have to do for the trial.

When I woke up in her bed this morning, I was just going to do my usual kiss to her forehead and quietly exit the house so I could get to my internship. But she'd been up with me and asked if she could come see where I work. Normally, I'd be completely opposed. Before I met Jolie, I knew I worked best alone, and that I'd never break the rules and bring someone unauthorized into the lab.

But the egotistical part of me wanted to show her what I was working on, even if I still hadn't told her why I was doing it. Each time I thought about bringing up my dad, like when I had a bad phone call with one of his therapists or just a tough exchange with my mom, I stopped myself. I want to lean on her for it, I do, but I know that it's my last line of defense. Once she knows about this, I'll be all in. She'll know all of my vulnerable secrets, the things I haven't allowed anyone else to see. I'm just about ready to take the plunge, but something is holding me back.

"Here's the grand operation." The lights flick on in the lab, and slowly everything seems to come to life.

It's a large room, separated by what is essentially a computer room and then a sealed off chamber for testing and specimen research. That room is almost all glass, so you can see into it, but I won't be taking Jolie in there today. On one side of the computer room is a bank of high-tech computers, microscopes, filing cabinets, and a bookcase of research textbooks. On the other side is a giant white board, which contains all sorts of scribbles and theories that any number of us throw up there throughout the days spent in here.

"Wow, it's not what I expected." She looks around.

"Is that good or bad?" I ask, setting my backpack and coffee down at the station I usually work at in the morning.

She shrugs, her hair piled on top of her head. She looks beautiful in the morning, all natural and fresh-faced. I prefer her like this, with no makeup in her sweats, I feel like I'm the only guy who gets to see her this way.

"For some reason, I was thinking it was going to look like a spaceship in here or something. I mean, it's impressive, but looks like an upgraded exam room at my doctor's office."

I snort. "Well, glad we can lower your expectations."

Jolie holds up her hands. "No, no, that's not what I'm saying. Honestly, I think it's ridiculously intimidating that you're a junior undergrad working on a medical trial. You're way smarter than I'll ever be, or probably anyone I'll ever know."

Firing up the bank of computers, I call her over. "Let me show you the latest discovery we think we found in DNA to possibly detect ALS."

As my computer gets up and running, I open a slide I'm really not supposed to be showing anyone who isn't involved in the trial, but it's just Jolie. It's not like she's going to tell anyone, much less care enough to understand all the jargon I'm about to throw at her.

I explain about the DNA sequence and a little about what the trial will involve for patients when it, eventually years down the line, gets approved by the CDC. She listens intently, and I know it's a lot to process, but I think I explain it well enough. I try to keep myself from getting too pumped up, because each time I think about it, I have to remind myself of the reality.

Dad could never get into this trial. It could not work for him, or a lot of patients like him. It could be years, which I don't know that we have with Dad.

When I tell her I need to answer some emails, Jolie wanders off, looking around the room.

She's across the room, examining something on one of the posters on the wall, when she clears her throat and catches my attention.

"This reminds me of our camp days, sneaking off to places we could almost get caught in." Jolie's smirk is erotic as she peeks through the curtain of her hair.

I know that look, the one that gets my blood heating and my cock stiffening. "Jolie, not in here …"

But she's not listening. She merely bends at the waist more, showing me the curve of her ass in those dangerous black yoga leggings.

This is exactly what I'm talking about. Before this girl, I would never be caught dead breaking a rule of any kind. I would strictly adhere to work and school standards and keep to myself above all that threatened to derail my goals or future.

But now she was in my life, and she'd painted it colors I never knew existed. It was as if she'd summoned my right brain out of its shell, eclipsing the rational left brain in me. And I just couldn't resist her, rationality be damned.

"Pull them down," I command, walking over to her.

Jolie's expression goes from playful to lust in two seconds flat.

"We don't really have to do this Mick, I was just kidding ..." She hesitates, and I'm almost over to the counter space she's leaning on.

"I said, pull them down." My face is deadly serious. "We have about thirty minutes before people start showing up for work, and I want you right here."

One of those fantasies I've had while choking the chicken, as Paul says, is having sex in the hospital I work in, or at work in general. Nudity under lab coats have been involved in these scenarios, but I don't have one and neither does she, so this will have to do.

Jolie doesn't think twice. In one fell swoop, she yanks down her leggings, underwear going with them, and then she's bare assed in front of me. Her spectacular, perky cheeks quiver under my gaze, and between her legs, I can see the glisten of how wet she already is.

When I reach her, I don't do more than pull my pants to my knees, leaving everything else in place. There is something dirtier about having sex with clothes on, something rushed and passionate about not having time to undress.

I've learned from numerous months with Jolie, not to mention the summer, to always carry a condom on me. You never know when we're going to try to go at it. Rolling it on hastily, I grab her hips and line myself up to her slit.

Fisting myself, I run my cock up and down her wet lips. "So ready for me. Is this why you wanted to come to work with me?"

My breath is on her ear and I feel the shiver go all the way down her spine. "Yes. I wanted you to fuck me in here."

The curse makes my nostrils flair, and I wrap her long brown hair around my hand, pulling it slightly. And before she can swallow the moan that elicits, I push in deep, sliding all the way into her slick heat.

"Oh my God ..." The plea comes out of her mouth, and I drive even deeper inside her.

This is what she does to me, makes me unravel, lose control. Except, in the strangest way, I feel more myself right now than I've ever felt.

Jolie doesn't fight me, in fact, she covers one of the hands gripping her hip with her own fingers, silently asking me to dig my digits in more. She juts up against me as I pull out slowly and then slam back into her.

All I want to do is destroy her, to act out every fantasy I've ever had about her, or fucking in the workplace.

I pummel my cock into her, over and over again. I hear myself snarling, and Jolie is matching me thrust for thrust.

Her head is thrown back, long brunette locks spilling down her back. The noises she's making are turning me into a wild animal, and if we're not careful, we're going to ruin highly pricey machines and computers. Her knuckles are white as she grips the counter with one hand.

I tear one hand off her hip, keeping my relentless, pounding pace into her, and reach up inside her long sleeve, to her bra. My finger find their way inside, tweaking at the perfectly budded nipples that I know are rosy pink whenever I blow on them. She gives a sharp cry.

"That's what you like, huh? This is what you wanted?" I taunt her.

I'm so close that it feels like my cock might break with all the pressure it's experiencing. "Come for me, Jolie. Come right here in this lab so I can think about it every time I step foot in this room."

"Mick!" she screams my name, and I clamp my hand over her mouth to stifle the shout.

When her pussy grips me hard with the first wave of her orgasm, I see white. I slam inside of her, just one hard, punishing thrust, and then I'm coming. I nearly black out from the bliss and hold on to Jolie like she's the last piece of shiplap from my sunken boat.

We've had some wild sex in some very kinky places, but I think this one takes the cake. I don't know how the hell she convinced the devil in me, the one only she seems to be able to summon to do this, but ...

I don't know how I'll ever work normally in this laboratory again.

30

That's the second time, I think to myself as I stare down at the screen of my phone.

Usually, I never send my mom to voicemail. Ninety percent of the time, our calls are just the regular family catchups with a few of Dad's checkups or therapies relayed to me over the phone.

But as I sit here next to Jolie in the library, and my phone is buzzing against my leg for the second time in two minutes, I know something is wrong. I have to answer it, but she's sitting right here.

"Can you excuse me for a minute?" I tell her.

Her head comes up slightly from where it was bent, focusing on her biology notebook. Her final is in less than two weeks, and we're in the home stretch. She's almost there, going to get through this first semester with passing grades, and I couldn't be more proud of her.

Her expression is puzzled, but she says, "Sure."

I stand up quickly, trying to weave my way through the second floor to a quiet nook.

"Mom?" I answer the phone quietly.

"Oh God, thank God, Mick. I thought you might be at the internship or class, I was panicking." My mom sounds frazzled.

"Is something wrong with Dad?" My stomach drops, waiting for her to confirm all of my worst nightmares.

"He's okay, for now. I'm calling because the insurance company won't cover that one medication again. They're fighting it, even with the doctor's note, prescription, and explanation. I don't know what to do. He's been on it for a while now, and I don't know the side effects of him going cold turkey. Or what it will do to his progress, he's had so much the past few months. I don't know what to do!"

Her voice is near hysteria, and I know the mental pain she's feeling right now. Dealing with the insurance companies has been one of the biggest pains in the ass with Dad's disease. They try to skirt out of paying for things that are clearly covered under our plan by using loopholes, percentages, making the doctors get ridiculous amounts of paperwork on why he needs a certain test or prescription ...

Anything under the sun they can do not to pay for things, they'll find it.

"Mom, okay, calm down. You're going to call Patricia over at the billing department of his neurologist. She knows exactly what is going on, because they've done this before. Then you're going to call Michael at the insurance company. Both of their numbers are in the drawer by the fridge. He's going to walk you through the proper steps you need to take, he knows our situation. I know this is frustrating, and if they say they can't get the prescription to the pharmacy for a couple of days, remind them of the detriment that could cause on Dad's state. They don't want their names in the papers, or worse, a lawsuit."

After dealing with some of the most malicious insurance agents and supervisors over the years, I've grown a thick skin when it comes to them. I know how to grease their wheels, push where I need to, and I've rigged the system to get my father what he needs. It blows my mind that the healthcare industry in this country actively wants to deny healing people.

Mom lets out a hiccupping sigh. "Okay, thank you. Thanks for calming me down, buddy. I just ... it's been hard without you here. We're the only two who have been in the trenches, you know?"

It might not be a typical thing a mother would say to her son, but I'd been more adult than a lot of people, including my mom, since a young age. And I know what she means.

"I know, Mom. I'm still here fighting alongside you, just in a different way now."

"Love you, Mick. Let me go call these people."

I tell her I love her, then we hang up. Leaning against a book-shelf in the dimmed corner of the library, I take a minute to control my emotions. I feel like I could lose it if I walk up to Jolie right now at that table, and I need to push the feelings down.

With each step I take back to the table, I feel the weight of my dad's illness and everything that comes with it like a boulder on my back. It's about to pin me to the ground, and Jolie must see it written all over my face when I sit down.

"What's wrong?" She reaches for my hand, concern marring her expression.

My gaze is focused down on the table, because this is new territory for me. I've never unloaded my family situation, or the burden it brings, on anyone else. I've kept these feelings locked inside, not even telling my parents how I feel most times because it would only make it harder on them.

"That was my mom. Um ... I've never really talked about this, so ..." I don't know where to start here.

Jolie squeezes my hand. "You can tell me anything. Please, Mick, I've never seen you this upset."

I take a deep breath before I step over the cliff.

"My dad was diagnosed with ALS six years ago. You know what that is?"

Jolie nods. "I sort of do. I mean, I know generally what it is, but not the full diagnosis of it. I'm so sorry, Mick."

She scoots her chair closer so that our knees touch; I have to swallow the lump of emotion that congeals in my throat.

"He's only gotten worse as time goes on. First, it was his ability to pick things up, simple things like a basketball or playing board games with my mom or me. His coordination began to slip, and then he started to limp. The muscles in his legs were weakening because of the disease, and within a year, he was walking with canes. Year two brought the wheelchair, and he couldn't walk anymore. That meant he couldn't drive a car, and then everything just got harder from there. Now he's bound to the chair, can't grab things with his hands, slurs his speech to the point where it's unintelligible, and can't even feed himself."

Jolie's eyes are misty as I talk, and I can tell she wants to hug me, but I have to get it all out.

"That's the reason I went to community college. I could have gone to my top choice, but the financial burden this is putting on my mom means she has to work so many jobs. My dad's disability and medical subsidies only pay for so much, and we couldn't get a full-time care nurse for him until this year. So I was his caretaker, and giving that up, even for my dream of college and medical school, has been extremely difficult. Especially when I can't be there if Mom has to take him to the doctor for an emergency. Or like right now, when the insurance company is denying a crucial medication and I can't be there to fight it with her."

"Jesus, Mick, I had no idea. I'm so sorry, you are and have taken on so much more than is ever asked of a normal college student." Jolie moves in to wrap her arms around me, and I let my head drop to her shoulder. "But you care, you want so fiercely to protect your dad and help your mom. That kind of love and loyalty is all they can ask for. I know you want to heal him, to make this all go away. I wish it could."

She just holds me for a while, in the middle of the quiet library. It's oddly comforting, when I didn't think I could ever feel relief telling anyone this enormous secret I'd been holding in.

"That's why you're working on the trial with Dr. Richards," Jolie murmurs to herself.

My eyes can't seem to meet hers, and I loll my head back down on her shoulder. "I begged to get on it when I got here. Dr. Richards is part of the reason I even came to Salem Walsh. I knew it was the best place to someday find a cure. I'm hoping to get into the medical school a year early."

"Mick, I ... I don't even have words. Your selflessness, your drive to try and help your family? You're one of the best people I've ever known. Probably *the* best. I'm so sorry. It doesn't seem fair that you or your father have to go through this."

It doesn't much matter what her words are at this moment, it's just that she's here. I've never had another person, outside of my family, experience this struggle with me. I feared for a long time that if I showed how scared it really made me, people would turn away. I'd seen it many times with doctors, nurses, physical therapists ... they clammed up if something was going wrong with Dad.

Jolie and I sit interconnected for a long time, and just having her touch makes my breath return to its normal rhythm, and the fear in my stomach go from panic level to its normal state of healthy concern.

Now that this barrier is down, that there is nothing between us, I feel like I could fall endlessly into this woman.

31

JOLIE

The secretary gives me a nod and says, "He'll see you now," before I'm rising to my feet.

When I got an email that the dean of Salem Walsh University wanted a meeting with me, I was equal parts scared and curious.

This could be about how well I've been doing, an update, if you will, on how my suspension is progressing. Or he could be throwing me out of the university altogether. I've stayed up nights worrying about this, and my hands begin to sweat as I press them into the professional black skirt I chose for this meeting.

Dean Wassak is a tall, slender man with a receding hairline and the fashion sense of Sherlock Holmes. He's always in weird, old English three-piece suits and I wouldn't be surprised if he pulled out a monocle at some point. He's sitting behind his massive desk, looking like a string bean compared to the palatial wooden furniture all around his office.

"Ah, Ms. Kenner, come in. Have a seat."

He points to one of two chairs across from his desk, but

doesn't rise. It's a power move, one I recognize from my father doing it countless times, and I shrug it off. I sit, reminding myself to keep impeccable posture and never to lose eye contact. If this old dude is about to throw me out on my ass, I'm not going down without a fight.

"The last time we met, it was under very unfortunate circumstances." He eyes me wearily.

Right. The last time I was in his office, I was dripping wet in little more than a T-shirt. "Yes. I sincerely apologize about that."

"I don't like seeing my students in distress, much less ones who have an active social life on campus and will go on to carry the Salem Walsh name prominently into the world."

What he's saying is that I come from money, and he wants the college on my résumé when I start job hunting.

"I can assure you, Dean Wassak, I've been keeping my nose clean and focusing on my studies."

His stern blue eyes assess me.

"I'm aware of that. With that being said, I don't see why, if you can't finish out this semester with a 3.8 GPA or higher at the community college, you can't come back as a full-time Salem Walsh undergrad next semester."

I honestly don't even believe my ears. I sit in stunned silence for a few moments, because I don't want to look like a moron and ask him to repeat himself.

"Sir ... thank you. I'm so appreciative. What ... I'm so thankful, but is there something that has happened?"

He swivels a bit in his high-back leather chair. "I've been keeping my eye on you, Ms. Kenner, and I'm impressed. You really seem to have turned it around from your previous semesters here at Salem. You haven't been written up once by campus police, have attended every class at the community college, and seem to be thriving with your grades. I'm not a cruel man, as much as people would like to make me out to be that way. I reward behavior that is exemplary."

A breath of pride fills my chest, because it's nice to hear that someone appreciates my efforts. "Thank you, Dean."

"Plus, you're from one of our brightest families and longest legacies. You deserve to be here, and I think the incident last school year really served to change your attitude and behavior."

My heart sinks a little. So, this is only partially because of my acceptance of the punishment and how well I've been doing. I haven't thought about it before, but I wonder how much my father has been pressuring Dean Wassak to lift my suspension and admit me as a student again. Now that I think about it, I would have never scored this much luck on my own. This had to have been a big boost from my father pressing his foot down upon the dean's neck.

At first, I want to rebuff his offer. I want to tell him I'll stay on the suspension for the entire year, because damn it if my father is going to be the one to win yet another battle for me. I've been working hard on my own, making sure I stay on the straight and narrow, and there is a chip on my shoulder.

But then I realize that chip does no one any good. How incredible would it be to have the weight of the suspension off my shoulders? To not have to lie to my best friends anymore? I could come back and take the much higher level courses offered at Salem and possibly score a big time internship for the summer. I wouldn't have to explain to any company hiring me for those three months about what my education situation was.

"Thank you, Dean. I am going to keep my grades up and hope to be able to transition back to Salem Walsh in the spring."

He nods, all but dismissing me. "Very well, we'll catch up after your finals. Please give your father my best."

It's my cue to leave, and I take it. I walk out of his office both elated and a touch disappointed. Even though my name and my background may have granted me this streak of luck, I was going to use it to carve my own path.

I'm determined now, more than ever, to get out from under my father's shadow.

Mick sits on my bed, flipping through the channels on my TV, as I curl my hair in the mirror above my dresser.

"Oh, this movie is great. You ever seen it?" he asks, lounging back on my pillows.

I peer over to see Denzel Washington in *Inside Man*. "Yes, such a good one."

"If I were ever to pull off a bank heist, that's the way I'd do it." He nods, self-assuredly.

I roll my eyes. "I could barely get you to have sex with me in a completely empty laboratory. I don't think bank robbing is really going to be on your docket."

He tosses one of my pink throw pillows at me. "You never know. Can't you see me as the bad boy?"

I look over my shoulder, the locks I've already curled moving with the motion, and scrutinize him. "Um, no. And I like it that way. The nerd in you turns me on."

"So come over here and show me." His legs fall apart.

"No, we're going out." I pout.

Mick snorts. "You can keep saying it, but as soon as you head to the party, I'm going back to the dorms to sleep."

I make a whining noise in the back of my throat, protesting. I've been trying to convince him all night that he should come out to this party with me, and he keeps refusing. We never go out together, but I have things to celebrate and I want my guy to come get drunk with me.

"Come on, come out with me. I passed my biology final! We have to celebrate that, and the fact that I could be a Salem Walsh student again by next semester."

I hadn't yet taken all of my finals, but my biology final grade was posted earlier today, and I'd gotten an A minus, which means I passed the course. If I could pull a couple more rabbits out of my hat, I'd be a Salem Walsh student next semester. I wouldn't ever have to hide my schedule from Christine and Madison. In fact, they'd never have to know. I could spend more time with Mick since I wouldn't have to be running back and forth between campuses.

And it would be a weight of guilt and shame off my soul.

"I won't be any fun, you really don't want me to come." Mick shakes his head.

The last lock of my hair falls through the curling iron, a perfect ringlet, and then I brush the whole thing out with my hands. Sauntering over to the bed in nothing more than my robe, I straddle his lap.

"Yes, you will. And yes, I really do want you to *come*."

Mick's sparkling green eyes heat to a deep olive color, and I know he's entranced. "You really want me to?"

"Let your hair down, Mr. Science. We both deserve it." I kiss him chastely.

Thirty minutes later, my Pub table group walks up the steps of one of the many sports houses on campus. We plan to start here and then travel down to the bars later on. I keep forgetting we can do that now that we're legal, because for so long it was water bottles full of vodka at house parties.

And Mick's hand is holding mine, my guy just one of our crew members. Granted, he's in his favorite dark jeans and an Apple logo T-shirt, but at least I got him out to a party.

"Let's start with shots." I smile deviously at him as soon as we walk in.

"It's your night, I'm just the puppet." He shrugs.

After his confession in the library, it feels like he's let his guard all the way down with me. He trusts me more than ever before, and I'm going to nurture that like it's a fragile egg I can't drop.

His secret, all the stress he's been carrying around ... it still shocks me. I can't believe that this man, so young in age, has taken on such a heavy and complicated role in his family's life already. I said it to him, but that kind of love and loyalty is unheard of in my family, and it's emotional to see. I can't get his expression out of my memory, that distraught, faraway look that said all he wanted to do was fix the problem.

My heart aches for his poor mother, dealing with all of this, and especially for his Dad. I can't imagine being diagnosed with a disease that steals everything from you. Mick's drive to find a cure is admirable, but I also worry. Will it devour him? He's already so dedicated and hyper-intelligent, so to hear him stress about everything on his plate just concerns me.

It's why I want him to let go of a little restraint tonight. I find two shot glasses and a bottle of whiskey, knowing he prefers it over vodka, and pour them out.

"To celebrating." I clink my glass against his.

Mick smirks and then tosses it back. "Ugh, Jesus, I don't know how people do this more than once."

I cackle. "Well, get ready, because we're about to do another."

I pour us two more, and we down them. The alcohol pulses

through my blood, heating me and making everything tingle. I'm ready to get into some shenanigans, though tamer ones than I usually participate in. I'm with Mick, and I'm happy he's here, but I'll keep the training wheels on this hot mess express for him.

"You want to play flip cup?" I suggest, spotting a table across the room.

Mick shrugs. "Sure, why not. I'm not very good, but it should be fun."

I take his hand and weave us through the crowded party. We join the game, and in the first two rounds lose terribly. I don't mind, it means we get to drink more. And the more we drink, the more giggly I get and the more handsy Mick gets.

"You're beautiful." He smiles down at me some time later when we're grinding our bodies together on the dance floor.

"And you're hot." I run a fingertip down his chest.

He ducks his head to whisper in my ear. "I'm serious, you're the most gorgeous creature I've ever laid eyes on."

My heart beats rapidly, and my spine tingles with him being so close. "You're making me blush."

"Good. The only thing I ever want to make you feel is cherished." He lands a kiss on the outside of my ear.

It's an interesting choice of words, because he doesn't say something that has to do with my appearance. Cherished implies a deeper connection, a bigger feeling. It's almost along the same lines as ... love.

"You do. Every day you do." I'm dead serious.

There we are, drunk in the middle of the dance floor at a house party, having the most serious conversation about us that we've had so far.

"I know I don't tell you often how much I care about you, but I do. I care about you more than anyone. Sometimes I don't think we need all that romance. I'm a practical guy, and you're a very confident woman. But I want you to know that. I ..." Mick pulls back so that I can look in his eyes.

He's about to say it, I know he is. Mick is about to tell me he loves me. But suddenly, we're shoved from behind by some rowdy assholes, and we tangle in each other as we shove the people behind us accidentally.

"Whoops." I giggle, as he helps me right myself.

"You okay?" Mick asks, and I see the seriousness still lingering in his eyes.

"I'm good. I feel like we need another drink!"

I'm scared, and I'm masking my feelings with the fun, cool girl persona I've always used as a crutch. If Mick tells me he loves me, I'm not going to be able to hold back from telling him the same. And even though we've come so far, I'm still terrified of that.

Mick lets me lead him back to the room where the alcohol is, and my hand seems to tremble in his. We're on the edge of the deepest commitment I've ever made to someone, and I'm just about ready for the fall.

Just give me one more night of fun.

33

The moment I open my eyes, I know something is wrong.

It's just that gut check, the one that feels like someone has socked you right in the pit of your stomach.

For starters, my mouth tastes like rotting fish, and my head is pounding as if I've been hitting it with a hammer all night. I've never really had a hangover, and this one is manageable as I try to sort through the fog of it, but I feel like absolute garbage.

When I roll over, trying to grab for a water, I see my phone. It lights up, and the time burns my retina.

7:20 a.m.

"Oh, shit!" I yelp, shooting straight up in Jolie's bed.

I fell asleep here last night after we stumbled home drunk, making love until the early hours of the morning. When Jolie convinced me to go out last night, I hadn't meant to get so wasted, but it felt so relieving to just let go for a few hours. With each shot she poured, with each game of pong and each song pumping through my veins on the dance floor, my problems seemed to melt away.

That's the issue with self-medicating though, whenever you

come down, the crash is always worse than the initial place or problem you were in.

I stumble over a shoe here, a purse there, and frantically search the ground for my clothes. I'm expected to be in the lab with Dr. Richards to go over test samples in ten minutes, and there is no way I'll make it there on time.

"Mick, what ..." Jolie's hair falls over her face as she leans up on her elbow. I woke her from where she was just sleeping on her stomach, and I can tell she's confused.

"I'm going to be late for my internship!" I hiss, annoyed at the entire morning.

I'm pissed off I slept late, I'm pissed off I went to that party, I'm pissed off that I could be so irresponsible when something so big is on the line. I promised Dr. Richards I could handle the internship with everything else I have going on, and now I'm going to let him down.

"What's the big deal? Come on, you're only going to be ten minutes late if you leave now." Jolie flips over in bed, smiling at me without a care in the world.

"You would say that," I mumble, shaking my head as I flit around the room like an angry wasp.

And something about her flippant attitude stings right under the surface of my skin. There she is, lounging in bed way past the time I get up every day, without any responsibilities or anyone to be beholden to.

"Huh?" Now Jolie sits fully up, puzzled. "What does that mean?"

I yank my shirt off the floor. "You know what it means."

"Actually, I don't. I get that you're late, but I didn't make you sleep in. Don't snap at me for something you're mad at yourself about." She gives me attitude, and now I'm seething.

"No, you just dragged me out to a party I didn't want to go to, and now are jeopardizing my internship," I shoot back.

Jolie's mouth falls open. "Are you freaking kidding me? We had a good time last night, and I didn't make you do anything you didn't want to. It's okay to be late for once in your perfect life, Mick."

The wire on the ticking time bomb that is my temper just about expires.

"You're a bad influence, Jolie! You parade around campus like some rich girl who has no responsibilities, and that's fine for you. But the rest of us have people counting on us, and goals to achieve, and we can't just spend Daddy's money and have him fix our problems."

I'm so mad now, I'm shaking as I pull on my clothes. I try to fix my hair as best I can in her mirror and grab my backpack.

I'm stomping through the house now, picking up my stuff as I go. One of my textbooks is on the kitchen table, my keys on the counter next to my student ID.

"You're seriously going to say that to me? You're being an asshole. I didn't force you to go out!" Jolie shouts at me, her white lacy nightie strap hanging off her shoulder.

I snort. "No, you just held the first shot glass to my lips and then promised sex. That's what you do, flaunt your curves and bat your eyelashes to get what you want!"

My blood boils as anger simmers within every muscle. I'm not seeing straight, and my fury is making me lash out, but I can't stop. I'm so fucking pissed at myself, at her, for breaking our initial agreement. We weren't supposed to fall into this; I told her from the start that I had serious goals and personal matters I needed to focus on. I promised myself I wouldn't become involved with her, and I knew that this was a possibility. I got too wrapped up in Jolie, in her aura, and I let myself be persuaded.

Just ten minutes is a big deal to me.

"You're being an asshole! You're late, suck it up, Mick. It

happens to us mere mortals all the time. I've never been anyone but myself with you, and you saying that, it really ..."

Jolie trails off, looking away from me, and I swear I hear her sniffle. Great, now she's crying.

"It really hurts. Let the freaking grips off your reins for a minute, apologize for being late, and that's the end of it. You're acting like a child!" Tears drip down her cheeks as she turns back to me.

And that's when I snap. Because she keeps insisting that the life I live is too rigid, too focused. She's the only one who knows how much I have to keep my nose down to get what my family needs, and she's acting like it's a casual lunch or something I'm running late for.

"The only child in this room is *you*." I point to her. "Going out every night of the week, when your future is on the line, too. No wonder you're in community college! Jolie Kenner, the girl with no obligations whose daddy will solve every mess. And even if he can't, you still can't seem to get your act together. I'm not going to let you take me down with you!"

A gasp comes from the other side of the kitchen, and I turn to see her roommates standing there. I realize, far too late, what I just said. What I just did. My stomach plummets, and a wave of enormous nausea slams into me.

"Jolie ..." My face must be a mask of sheer panic as I try to reach for her.

She shoulders away, wrapping her arms around herself. "Get the hell out."

"I didn't, that wasn't—"

"Get out of my house!" she screams, the veins in her neck popping.

I should stay here, apologize, talk this out, but I don't have time. I have to get to the hospital, to the place I'd freaked out about getting to in the first place.

Grabbing my things off the counter, I hastily run out of the house, regret and anger following me the entire way.

I probably just lost the only girl who will ever love me the way Jolie does, and yet ...

My mind is still focused on my future and finding a cure for my father. I knew going into this, way back when I warned myself to stay away from Jolie, that I'd give anything and everything up to heal him.

And now, my premonition has just come true.

34

I don't leave my room until two p.m.

I wish I could say I was sleeping that entire time, but mostly I was crying. And trying to figure out what to text Mick to make things right. Or what to text him out of the horrendous anger chewing me up inside.

My eyes feel raw, and when I look in the mirror before heading for the door, it looks like I've popped a few blood vessels in them.

I can't believe that all happened so quickly, that it went down the way it did. We had the best time at the party last night, and, I thought, we were really getting closer. Not to mention we spent the wee hours of the morning screwing each other's brains out.

And then, before I was even roused from my full REM cycle, Mick had freaked out so badly that the damage was likely irreparable. I guess I hadn't been listening to him about how worried he was in terms of being late, but the things he'd said to me ...

They can't be taken back. He called me every name I've always internalized and resented. The things he said about me were so ugly that I feel like he slashed my confidence, my self-worth and my heart in half. Everything inside me aches with sadness and fury. I have no idea how we come back from this.

This is never what I meant to happen. I never meant for us to pick up where we left off at Camp Woodwin, or for it to get so serious. I never thought I'd fall in love with Mick Barrett. Yet here I am, heartbroken the way all the books and love songs describe it.

Scrubbing my hands down my face, I turn from the mirror. No use in focusing on that now. I walk out in search of food, though I'm not actually hungry. My stomach is rumbling, and I'll see if I can manage a few bites of toast.

Christine and Madison stand in the kitchen, holding mugs that look like tea.

You know that feeling when you stumble into a room and you realize someone is talking about you? Or someones are talking about you? Yeah, I get that icy cold nail of dread dragged directly down my spine the minute I enter the kitchen.

I'm already not in the mood to talk to them, being so distraught over what happened with Mick this morning. It doesn't matter though, because they start in on me immediately.

"What the hell happened this morning?" Madison asks, coming over with a concerned look on her face.

"I don't want to talk about it." I pull down my loaf of bread from the cabinet and busy myself making toast.

"Jolie, we heard you all screaming at each other at seven a.m. We want to make sure you're okay ..." Maddy keeps at it.

"I'm fine." I sniff, throwing out the line every woman produces when she is so very far from fine.

"Psh, that's a company line if I've ever heard one. You're not fine. Talk to us. Mick said some pretty ugly things," Christine chimes in, and I really don't want to hear from her at this moment.

I snort snidely as my toast cooks. "No shit, you think? Why

do we have to do a download about the entire fight? You heard what he said. He was pissed off that we partied and he ran late for his internship. Apparently I'm irresponsible, have no goals, and I'm not worthy of a smart guy like him."

He didn't say that, but it was all but implied.

"None of that is true, you know that." Madison comes up behind me and wraps her arms around my waist.

I shrug her off, because I don't want anyone touching me right now. I can't bear it. Something inside me has broken. It's like all the insecurities I've ever felt about myself, Mick just held them up one by one and confirmed. Typically, I don't give a shit what people say about me. But he's the one person I've ever really opened up to. Mick knows all of my biggest secrets, vulnerabilities ... even more than my family or my best friends.

"What did he mean about community college?" Christine's tone is laced with curiosity and prying.

I knew it. I knew she wouldn't let that go. Even if I'm in the most horrible breakup of my life, she won't stop digging.

"You would ask that. He just tore me down and I've been crying for hours, but that's all your focused on." I turn around, practically spitting the words at her.

She holds her hands up helplessly. "We both had no idea what he was talking about, so what is going on? Are you going to community college?"

There is no way I'm getting into this discussion right now. I've already had one blow out today, I have no energy to do it again.

The toast pops up, and I pull it out, all but burning my fingers. "Why don't you just add onto my stress for the day?"

"Jolie, I'm not trying to do anything, but we're worried. What the heck is going on?" Christine pushes, and I'm at my breaking point.

"Yes, I'm going to community college. There, that good for you?" I throw my hands up, my temper flaring.

"What? Why? I thought you were in all of those courses on campus ..." Madison tilts her head to the side, so confused.

I stay silent, buttering my toast even though there is no way I can eat it at this point. The girls are quiet behind me, until I hear Christine clear her throat.

"This is about the fountain, isn't it? You didn't skate out of punishment; this is what happened. You were ordered to go there for the semester?"

Her guessing so close to the truth is what makes me snap.

"Welp, guess you figured that one out, Christine. How long have you been snooping around? I'm sure it's not the first time you've thought something weird was going on. Yes, Daddy couldn't fix this one for me, and you all left me to get picked up alone. I didn't say even one of your names, but that wouldn't have stopped you from berating me about community college, would it? You want to know why I didn't tell you? Because I knew I'd get the holier than thou, Christine talk about how I'd fucked up. Or maybe you would have gone the route of why my spoiled princess ass couldn't just pay off whatever punishment it was? Is that what's running through your mind?"

"No one is saying that, girl." Madison tries to give me a hug.

"Don't." I hold up a hand.

Christine looks stricken, but it doesn't mean she hasn't thought those things. "Jolie, I'm ... I would never want you to be in that situation. How can you even think that? I hate that you thought you couldn't tell us that."

I blow out a frustrated breath. "Because I don't get to have problems, remember? Every time I try to vent, I'm told that I have money, so it shouldn't be that big of a problem. Or some sort of judgment like that. After a while, I just started playing my part like you all wanted me to."

Leaving my toast abandoned on the counter, I stomp back to my room and slam the door.

I have nowhere to go, no one to turn to. I don't want to stay in this house, the one that has always felt the closest like home.

For the first time in a very long time, my desire to return to my family home is actually something I feel in my soul. I need to get away from Salem Walsh, to lick my wounds, to mourn.

But damn if my world doesn't feel so fucking lonely right now.

The house is quiet, nothing on but an old rerun of a *Real Housewives* franchise on my TV.

I'm lying upside down on my bed, my head hanging off the end so that my vision is up into the canopy hanging high above. It's how I spend most days, never leaving this California king, and I'm so sad I could just shrivel up into a ball.

It's been two weeks since I came home for winter break, and I've barely seen another human being. My parents were home for the first six days, just until after Christmas, and then jetted off to Milan. When they asked if I wanted to come with them, I thought about it. I really did. An international escape sounded like the perfect medicine for me right now.

But then I thought about what Dean Wassak said, and how Christine regarded me when I said my father couldn't fix the mistake I'd made last year. By getting on that plane and trying to throw money at my heartbreak, it would only perpetuate the issue. I'd be doing the exact thing I'd always felt so judged for, and I didn't want to spend any more time with my parents.

Before my fights with Mick and my best friends, I'd been determined to carve my own path outside of my family name.

Staring up at the four-poster bed, I try to strain to hear any signs of life. My bedroom at my childhood home is bigger than four dorm rooms at Salem Walsh put together, and my mother has redone it for the fiftieth time, in taupes and beiges so muted that I feel like I'm living inside a pair of khaki pants. There is nothing *me* about this room, and nothing human about the house in general. It's a museum, a shrine to architecture and clean lines, rather than a family home that makes you feel warm and comforted the minute you step in the door.

But the peace and quiet gives me time to cope. To think about the utter disaster that is the organ in my chest. To swallow what Mick had said to me, and how I'd treated both him and Madison and Christine.

What he said to me was horrible, but I wasn't without blame. I hadn't listened to him when he said he didn't want to go out. I thought I was doing something good for him, but I forgot about what he'd confessed to me. He'd leaned on me about why he worked so hard, about why he pushed himself into the internship, about his father's disease. I should have considered it more, calmed him down and gotten to the core of it rather than being so flippant.

What I did was bad, but what he did was worse. Which was why I hadn't responded to his call, or the message he'd sent me. I could tell, from both, that he was still pissed off at me, too. But he was apologetic as well, for lashing out and calling me those ugly names. And from his message, he was sorry about spilling the community college secret to my roommates.

He was the reason that I was in a fight with my roommates as well. Not that we were exactly fighting, because they'd only sent me sympathetic, concerned texts since we'd been home. Ones I also hadn't returned. I didn't know what to say. I didn't think I could tell them about the suspension, because I didn't want to be judged. No one in my life had ever comforted me, and I was afraid they wouldn't have done that either. I see now, with their words and actions, that they probably would have, but I'm too wounded.

And I miss them all like crazy. Especially Mick. I miss talking to him, even about the dumbest parts of our days. I wonder every second about what he's doing, if he's having a tough time at home with his father's health. I wonder if he got in trouble with Dr. Richards, and if he's as upset as I am.

I wonder if he's so heartbroken that he can barely get out of bed, or barely eat. I wonder if he closes his eyes when his head hits the pillow and sees memories of us.

There has never been another time in my life I've been this melancholy. Which I guess means I am spoiled, or blessed, or all the other things people like to heap on girls like me.

A yearning ache in the pit of my stomach wants to end this sadness, to reach out to everyone, but there is something stopping me. With Madison and Christine, it will fade. My frustration has all but dissipated with them, it's just pride holding me back now. I shouldn't have snapped, but I'd reached my breaking point and they'd pushed me.

When it comes to Mick, I just can't answer him. He hurt me worse than anyone ever has, or will ever have the power to. As deeply as I miss him, as much as I've fallen in love with him, I'm not sure I can get past this.

So here I sit in this silent house, more alone than I've ever been.

More heartbroken than I ever will be again.

"Mick, I'm going out for a bit. You're sure you'll be okay?"

Mom calls from the front hallway of our house, and I know she's stalling.

I poke my head out from around the living room wall. "Yes, Mom, now go. You deserve it."

Dad and I got her a spa gift card for Christmas, that she has yet to use in the almost three weeks I've been home. She rarely gets to do anything for herself, and with a rare day off of work, and me home to watch Dad, she should take this time to recharge her batteries.

"Okay, I'll be home in an hour or so. I love you. Call me if you need anything!" Her voice is tinged with worry, but I hear her open the front door.

"We love you!" I call from my seat on the old brown leather couch.

When Dad and I hear the front door close, I turn to him. "I thought she'd never leave."

His smile is lopsided but genuine, and I've missed this. As stressful as it is being home and dealing with all of Dad's needs,

I've missed time with my parents. Our house sits on a cul-de-sac, a two-story brick Cape Cod style with a screened in front porch. It's filled with worn-in furniture, tables with nick marks on them, rugs that I've burned holes in with my middle school chemistry set. In my bedroom, the walls are plastered with posters of *Battlestar Galactica*, *The Office*, and *Star Wars*. It's not the fanciest place on earth, but it's home, and when I walk in the front door, I can always smell the scent of Mom's homemade cooking or the fresh daisies she always keeps on the hall table.

It's been nice to be home, to get out of the grind of classes and the internship and worrying about my parents while I can't physically be in my hometown. Mom and I spend time cooking together, and she's even taken a few days off her crazy schedule. Dad, surprisingly, looks better than I've seen him in years, though the progress is slow and it's just a standstill on his quality of life, really. What most people would consider good health ... Dad will never have that again. But the more we can prolong the decline of his disease, to hopefully find a cure, the better chances he has.

There is a football game on our years old TV, a sport I don't even know all the rules for, but Dad enjoys it so I sit here with him. Back when he could talk without so much effort, he'd talk to me about plays and routes and the like, and I'd just sit here and let him talk at me. I wish, now, that I'd soaked more of it up so I could regurgitate it back to him.

"How"—Dad gulps—"is school?"

"School is good, great honestly. Really challenging, but in the best way possible. I'm learning a lot in my classes, and I'm hoping I can fit them all in so that I can go to medical school next year. The internship is mind blowing. The things Dr. Richards is working on are just insane, next level stuff. I can't wait until the trial is in its early stages, to see if his theories will actually work."

Dad nods his head—the slightest, imperceptible movement —as if to show me he's listening.

"And … friends?"

He's asking about my social life when he says this.

I shrug. "Yeah, my roommates are nice enough. We talk and sometimes hang out."

"Gi-girl?" He smirks as well as he can.

My breath whooshes out, because I have a feeling Mom's been talking to him. I made the mistake of picking up one of her phone calls with Jolie in the room, and she heard her in the background. Mom had six billion questions, none of which I answered, and now I'm sure she's put Dad on the case to dig up some dirt.

Too bad there is no dirt to dig. Unless they want to know that their son is just as big of an asshole as every other jock and bad boy on the Salem Walsh campus. The things I said to her, the way I tore her down to justify my own temper tantrum.

They're unforgivable.

Yes, I'm pissed at how flippant she was, but I was the worse one out of the two of us. I called her every name that she's always wanted to scrub off her, and now I can't take them back. She thinks I think that of her, when I was in a selfish blind rage just trying to lash out. There has been so much pressure on my back that I snapped, and it was at the only girl I've ever loved.

She hasn't responded to my one call or heartfelt message I sent, and I don't expect her to. I broke her trust in the worst way possible and managed to out her secret to her roommates. But it doesn't mean I don't miss her every damn second of the day. And it burns me every day that I never got to tell her exactly how I feel about her, that I put other things in front of her.

It's what I said I'd always do, put my goals and dreams ahead of anything else, but falling in love with her shifted my entire vision.

"Yeah, there is no more girl." I try not to meet his eyes, but his silence is blaring.

Looking at Dad, his green eyes, the same as mine, penetrate my soul. I know he's looking for more, and I sigh, rolling my own eyes.

"There was someone, yes. We actually ... we met at the camp I worked at and she ended up going to Salem Walsh. At first, it was just casual—you know I'm no ladies' man. And she's ... her name is Jolie, she's the most beautiful girl I've ever seen. There is no way she'd pick me out of a lineup. We kept hanging out and spending more time together, but I made it clear that my studies and my internship came first. Anyway, I let those things get in the way in the long run, because I chose them over her. I said some things that I can't take back, and now it's done."

I set my head in my hands, because just talking about it makes my heart crack into a million pieces.

A noise, like someone clearing their throat, makes me pick it back up.

Dad motions for me to get his water, and I put the straw in his mouth. He takes a long chug, and his eyes don't leave mine. When he releases the straw, I put it back on the table, and he takes a ragged, deep breath.

"I want ... to tell ... you ... something, son." He says the words, but they're jumbled and it takes him a while to get them out.

My initial reaction is to lay a hand on his arm, to tell him to stop, don't strain himself. But he looks so serious, so determined, that I hold off. Plus, I haven't heard his voice, no matter how slurred, in too long.

"Love is ev ... everything. Fuck work ..." He takes a long, deep breath, and I have to chuckle because I don't think I've heard him curse in years. "Fuck cures. All ... that mat- matters is that person ... beside you."

I want to argue with him, show him that all I'm doing, when keeping my nose to the grindstone, is for him. But he shakes his head the slightest bit.

"Get ... her b-back. At ... all costs." He lets out a wheezing, heavy breath.

He's done speaking, and I let that sink in a moment. Here he is, slowly losing his life, but all he cares about is that I have someone like Mom by my side in the long run. The thing is, I've been thinking the same thing myself. Because while my life used to revolve around theories, test scores, grades, and education, the only thing occupying my mind is Jolie.

I see her face every time I go to sleep, and every time I wake up. The word love runs through my mind a thousand times a day, and it burns me up inside that I didn't tell her.

I'm not sure how I'm going to make it right, but if this is the piece of advice Dad is taking his painstaking time to give, then I'll follow it.

One way or another, I have to get her back.

Even though I was glad to go home for the holidays, I'm even more happy to be back at school.

As I drive through campus on the way in, nostalgia hits me from every angle. This has been my home for three years now, and after next year, I'll have to leave it. This is the place I realized I could grow into a person I actually wanted to be. This is the place where I could have a fresh start, where my family name didn't have to precede me at every turn.

With its winding path through the ivy-covered buildings and the whip of wind through the leaves on the ground, I open my windows and inhale deeply. A calmness that hasn't occupied my soul in nearly a month washes over me, and I have a feeling everything is going to be okay.

Especially since I'm a Salem Walsh University undergrad, officially, once again. Dean Wassak sent me an email over break that my finals scores were good enough to allow my enrollment back on campus, and I couldn't be happier. With that ugliness behind me, I can finally start acting the way I should have before any of it even happened.

I'm glad it did, though. It taught me some invaluable lessons, and I met Mick along the way.

We didn't speak for the entire four weeks of winter break, and it gave me time to clear my head. While I don't regret a second of what happened between us, aside from that blowout fight at the end, I do realize now that we moved extremely fast. As is normal in a college relationship, because you have access to each other twenty-four seven, we got too wrapped up in each other. He was choosing me over things that really mattered to him, and I was falling in love without looking first.

It's probably for the best if we cool off, if I focus on my studies and nabbing an internship for the summer.

Turning my car down the street that leads to our little ranch off campus, I breathe a sigh of relief when I see the driveway empty. I wanted to be the first one back, to gather my wits before Christine and Madison got there. We've texted a few times over break, mostly to just apologize and clear the air, but this will be the first real face-to-face moment.

After I park in the spot I always take in our driveway, I begin to unload my car. Who the hell knows how I could possibly need more stuff packed into my tiny college room, but I brought back enough to clothe and feed an army.

I'm lugging a box up and into my room when Christine appears around the corner. We look at each for a moment and then walk quickly toward each other. I throw my arms around her, and she does the same.

"I'm so sorry," she sobs.

"I am, too." I sniffle into her hair.

We hug each other hard, and I know right then and there that we're going to be just fine.

"I was an asshole, pushing you like that when you'd just gone through a breakup. I should have comforted you, given you ice cream, let you cry it out over a sappy episode of *One Tree Hill*," she explains, pulling back.

I shake my head. "No, no, I should have told you guys from the start. You're my best friends. I was just terrified of what you would think. And I didn't want to be judged, I just wanted to do my time and then get back to living my regular life. The more people who know, the more real it made it. And I should have told you what was happening with Mick, I was such a bitch."

"No, that all makes perfect sense. You're okay now though, right? I mean, you're back?"

"Officially a Salem Walsh student once again." I grin, and we high five.

Just then, Madison walks in carrying a forty-eight pack of toilet paper. "What's going on in here?"

"We're having makeup sex," I deadpan.

"No fair, I'm horny, too!" She drops the toilet paper and bounds over to us, grappling us into a tight group hug.

I breathe them in, getting emotional. "I missed you guys. I'm really sorry."

"No, I'm sorry, too," Madison sobs. "Let's never fight again?"

"Never." Christine swears, and then backs up. "All right, enough. We're acting like sappy sorority girls."

I crack up along with Maddy, and it's really nice to have my two friends back.

My mood is infinitely improved after we all have a "welcome back" glass of wine together, and we promise to meet up in the living room to watch the latest episode of some cheesy Netflix show after we all unpack.

So I'm not expecting it in the least when Madison comes to my room and tells me there was a knock at the door ... for me.

I give her a puzzled look, but she just scurries off. So I head for our front door, and when I spot who it is through the glass, my heart drops.

Mick stands on our front porch, looking as devastating as he ever has. Did he grow a beard over Christmas? God, I hate that I almost go weak at the knees.

Slowly, I open the door, trying to keep my face neutral. For four weeks, I've cried and sulked over this guy. I've thought about him endlessly, and this is exactly what I've wanted to happen. I wanted him to come crawling back, though I'm not sure that's exactly what he's doing. And now that he's here, my heart is beating on overdrive. But I forgot all the things I'd planned to say.

"Can we talk?" Mick ducks his head, and his eyes are apologetic.

I nod, scared out of my mind for what's to come, but knowing that there is another talk that needs to be had today.

It's just that this conversation is the hardest one I'll probably ever have, and it could break my heart irreparably.

38

MICK

When I decided to show up at her house, hoping she'd have gotten back to campus already, I didn't know if Jolie would agree to talk to me.

But I made Dad a promise, that I'd try at all costs to get her back, and that's what I'm doing. I want to show Jolie that she's the first thing I thought of when I got back to campus. I want to tell her she's the only thing I've thought of since the day I stormed out of her house.

We walk in silence just a little ways down from her house, where there is a small playground with some park benches. I've seen this park once or twice and always thought it was odd because why would a street full of rundown college houses require a children's playground? But I guess if there is someone mature who lives in the vicinity, they need a place to take their kids. Hopefully, it's just not littered with beer cans, or condoms.

I take a seat on one of the benches, and Jolie sits too, but keeps a healthy distance between us. Man, she looks as stunning as ever. Her skin, though it's the middle of winter, looks sun-kissed, and she's fresh-faced. I love her best like this, when I can see the natural curve of her lashes against her cheeks, and the slight blush her cheeks naturally carry. She's gorgeous and raw, and I wish I could hold her.

But I don't reach out, because I know better. I can't mess this up. We've fallen into the mistake of going right to the physical too many times before. This time, there needs to be words before action.

"Thanks for agreeing to talk to me." I try to maintain eye contact with her, but it's hard.

My heart is sprinting a lopsided race. It feels like a horse at the Kentucky Derby on its last leg. I want to get to the end, to make it whole and nab a victory, but I know I have to go through the pain first.

"I've been wanting to reach out, it just felt ..." She stops herself from saying whatever it is that she was going to.

I nod, like I've filled in those words. "First off, I need to say how sorry I am. I was so out of line, the way I spoke to you. Those words were ugly and not true at all. They were said in the heat of my anger, and that is no excuse, and I'm just so sorry, Jolie. I burn with shame every time I think of the things I said to you."

Her mocha orbs meet mine, and thankfully I don't detect any malice in them. "Thank you for that. Honestly, they really hurt, those words. I confided in you, told you how much of those were insecurities of mine. It felt like you were personally tearing down everything I've tried not to be. I've been trying really hard this year to right the wrongs I've committed, and to have you, someone I really care about ..."

Jolie breaks off, as if her explanation is too emotional for her to continue.

I jump on the empty air. "And I swear, I didn't mean a single word. I snapped, with all of the things on my back, and I took it out on you. You're the one person who knows everything about me, and I used it as a weapon against you. I'm so sorry, Jolie."

She tilts her head to the side, lost in thought. After what feels like a year, she speaks.

"I get it, I really do. I can't begin to imagine the stress you feel on a daily basis. I understand why being late set you off like that. I wasn't right that morning either. I shouldn't have brushed off your feelings, and probably should have listened to you the night before when you said you didn't want to go out."

"None of this is on you." I shake my head. "It took me about three seconds to come to that realization. And then it took my dad knocking some sense into me to realize this. That I ... I'm in love with you, Jolie. I've thought of nothing else since I left your house that day, and even more when I went home for break. I love everything about you. I love that you break me out of my comfort zone, that we're so different and you don't seem to care at all. I love the way you don't let what other people think about you affect you, and your individualism inspires me. You're so bright and whip-smart, two things that you sometimes hide in favor of blending in. I love that I get to see you in your most natural state, and that I could be the only one to make you smile in the morning—even if you haven't had your coffee. I know I have so much to apologize for, but I can't go another minute without telling you how in love with you I am. As my dad says, it's all that matters. None of this other stuff means one thing if I don't have it with you by my side."

I had no idea I would take that moment to blurt out all of my feelings, but there it is. Once I thought it, it all tumbled out, and I'm glad it did. She needs to know how I feel, even if this is our last conversation.

The gorgeous woman in front of me, *my girl* once upon a time, looks like I've just dropped an atomic bomb right in front of her. She couldn't look more shocked if there were an alien standing in front of her telling her that it was from the year three thousand and twenty-five.

"Mick ... I ..." Her long, vanilla-scented locks whip in the wind as she looks down into her lap. "I feel like I've waited for a while to hear something like that. And it's so ... I can't even form words."

I give her a minute to collect her thoughts, but inside, I'm panicking. My heart is in flux, and every nerve ending in my body is spazzing out.

"I had a lot of time to think about this over break, and I really do forgive you. What we had was special, and it was the most important relationship I've probably ever had. But ... maybe we were right in the beginning, especially you. You have a lot on your plate, and we are very different people. I think things went too quickly, and you have so many important goals and dreams that I don't want you to lose focus on. I don't mean any of this in a bad way, and I really appreciate everything you've said, it means more than you know. I think for right now we should pump the breaks a little. I'm fully back at Salem Walsh, so we can see each other freely. You have so much coming up with the internship, I'm sure, and I need to focus on landing one for the summer."

She's forgiving me, but the whole thing feels unresolved. I know that Jolie is being genuine when she says she doesn't harbor any resentment, but it doesn't mean she loves me back. At the end of the day, the things she's not saying, or possibly doesn't feel cut deeper than accepting my apology for my behavior. I told her I loved her and she isn't going to say it back.

Maybe I jumped the gun on professing my feelings, but like Dad said, at all costs. I laid it all out on the line, and that's all I could do. She all but pushed it back into my hands, refusing to take the hot potato, but I didn't wuss out and I stayed true to my feelings.

I'm proud and heartbroken, all at the same time.

"So, not never, but not right now." It comes out as a statement, and I'm not sure I mean it as a question.

Jolie shrugs. "I think we always seem to jump before we look, so let's try it the opposite way this time. If anything, that's one of the biggest lessons I've learned this year."

She leans in, so close that I could taste her lips if I moved my head at the right angle, and blinks slowly. I think maybe she's about to change her mind, but at the last second she presses a lingering kiss to my cheek. Then she stands and carefully backs away, before she turns back to her house.

I'm left on the bench alone, not sure if I should be hopeful or decimated.

39

JOLIE

I've gone over the conversation in my head a thousand times and doubted what I said triple that.

I'm proud of me, for sticking up for myself. But was turning him down the right thing to do? Should I have told him I loved him back? I just don't know. I've argued with myself too many times to count in the last two weeks, and can't come up with the right answer.

Madison and Christine tell me I should run back to him, confess my love and live happily ever after. I'm surprised that critical, rational Christine is agreeing with our rose-colored glasses friend, but she's always been a Mick lover. She said I've been punished enough, and that I deserve my happy ending.

Maybe that's true, but I've also kind of liked spending time with myself, as a single person. I've always been involved with someone, whether it was a fling or more serious, and taking this break through Christmas and up until now has given me some time to really get reacquainted with myself.

And the biggest factor of all? I'm terrified. Terrified of being rejected again, about fully opening my heart to him and him whacking it with a two-by-four, like he did before winter break. I know he said all of those beautiful things, but it doesn't fully rub clean the wound he left when he spit all those ugly things at me. I was utterly shocked when he told me he loved me, because I never saw it coming. I'm the impulsive, emotional one. Mick is the logical, down-to-earth, sometimes distant one. It must have taken a lot for him to tell me how much he truly cares, but I'm gun-shy. I want to pull the trigger, go running back to him, but I can't seem to do it.

I usually take my beach walks at the end of a semester, to clear my head and put me on the right path before I go back to my parent's palatial prison. But when I woke up this morning, the ocean was calling me, and so here I am.

My toes dig into the sand as I stroll along, with no real purpose or direction. It feels good to wander, to let the sea salt answer my questions and heal my hectic thoughts. It's still pretty chilly, it being January, but I don't mind. Facing the ocean, I wrap my sweater around myself and gaze out over the waves.

The ocean has a hypnotic quality, one that sucks you in and clears your mind of all worry. For me, it's better than meditation, which I can never do because I can't turn my brain off.

It's so calming that I almost miss the motion out of the corner of my eye, but then I turn. This beach is typically empty, especially this time of year, so I'm startled to be sharing it with someone else.

And when I catch who it is, I'm even more surprised.

"Mick!" I say in disbelief.

His back is turned, because I think he saw me standing here and had an "oh, shit" moment. He's literally scurrying away like a teenage girl who just saw her crush and is too nervous to go up and talk to them. Only here, we're the only ones on this beach and it's extremely obvious he saw me and decided to take off in the other direction.

I stomp after him, sand flying up behind me. "Mick, wait!"

When I get within a good distance of him, he finally turns on his heels and stops in front of me.

Mick holds his hands up in defense, as if I might start yelling at him. "I swear I didn't know you were here. I just wanted to come clear my head and thought you only came here at the end of the semester. I truly didn't—"

I cut him off. "Relax, I'm not going to freak out on you. This a public beach, and anyone can come here. But especially because we left things in a good place. I meant what I said, I forgive you. I honestly think it's funny we're here at the same time."

As if I hadn't just been basically asking the ocean for answers to my problems.

He studies my face, as if he's trying to memorize us both here. It breaks my heart at the same time that it sends it soaring.

"I came here because I wanted to feel closer to you. To think about how good we were before I screwed it all up. I'm sorry, I'm invading your space. This is your spot where you come to be alone. I'll go."

He's about to turn when I blurt it out. "I love you."

Mick stutters, almost falling over on himself, because I think I utterly bamboozled him. I bamboozled myself, because I had no idea that was about to come out of my mouth. Apparently, the beach and waves are making decisions for me and then using me as their mouthpiece. *Literally.*

"What ..." Mick's eyes, the color of the deepest green out in that ocean, search mine.

I shrug, trying to come up with an explanation as to why I just had word vomit. I wrack my own brain, because what the heck is going on inside me. The minute I saw him walking away from me on this beach, my beach, *our* beach, I just knew. I'd been wavering back and forth for weeks, too scared to admit it to myself or anyone and yet still longing to get back together and live in happiness with him.

"I ... I do. I love you." I smile weakly, because the realization slams into me the minute I speak to the words aloud to him. "My entire life, I've lived on a whim. Following every impulse, diving head first into anything I wanted. And when it came back to bite me, take a dinosaur-sized chunk out of my life, I knew I had to change. Over the past year, I've learned not only who I am as a woman and a person, but what I want out of my relationships with other people. I've learned that I am capable of much more than I could have possibly thought, including standing on my own two feet and fighting for myself. It's made me more cautious, with less of a penchant for trusting my natural instinct of jumping before I look. But when I saw you here, it was like ... the world gave me a sign. I can still have some of that impulse, while balancing it with all the things I've learned in the last year. So, I love you. I've been going back and forth for weeks, since you came to my house to talk, wondering if I should tell you. I can't imagine we ended up here at the same time by coincidence."

Mick is staring at me with such intensity that it feels like I'm basking on the surface of the sun.

"You love me," he says, before taking the two steps between us and pulling me fiercely to him.

Our mouths meet in the middle, fighting to get closer and closer to each other. The kiss ignites me, burning every pore and cell. The cold wind whips around us, but I might as well be a volcano erupting with the heat and passion Mick is heaping upon me.

"I love you," I answer, not that he asked a question.

"I love you," he breathes, going back in for more as our lips collide.

Before my suspension, before meeting Mick, I would have never questioned something so cliché and perfect. I would have said that this kind of chance meeting was how love, or lust, worked, and followed my gut.

Right now, at this moment, is no different.

Because I know that this moment isn't cliché. It isn't perfect. It took a lot of stumbles and hard conversations and real, raw moments to get here. When it came down to it, both sides of me helped the other to tell this man how I really feel.

And now, we can start our honest, sometimes hard, sometimes beautiful happily ever after.

40

In the month since Jolie and I reunited on the beach, life has been sweeter than ever.

There is something grounding in the fact of knowing where your relationship stands. Now that we've both said those three big words to each other, our connection and depth seems unbreakable. There are no questions about what we are, she is my woman and I'm her man. Yes, when we're in social situations, we use the terms boyfriend and girlfriend, but it feels like so much more than that.

I feel more centered than I've ever been. Dad was right in that, of course, he was. With her by my side, without any doubts or hesitation, life just seems easier. We both still have bad days, obviously, but I find that courses are easier to get through. When I get home from a long day at Dr. Richards' lab, she's there to comfort me. When I get a negative update from Mom, Jolie is the one I can lean on to power through the worry and stress.

We're so different, and it helps to have two opposite personalities in one relationship. Jolie sees things from a point of view that I don't, or can point out where I'm being too jaded. And in turn, I bring her back down to earth sometimes. She injects the fun, and I bring the rationality, and together it actually makes a great combo.

I knew I wanted to do something nice for her since this is our first Valentine's Day together, but I'm nervous because I've never taken a girl on a date. Much less one who is my girlfriend.

"Will you relax? I've never had a Valentine's Day with a boyfriend either." Jolie squeezes my hand as we walk through the downtown near our college.

I swear, sometimes she can read my mind.

"I just think you'll really like this place." My spine sparks with anxious energy.

Jolie smiles up at me, the pink dress she's picked hugging every curve of her luscious body. I steer us toward a restaurant on the main strip, its windows decorated in red and pink hearts. Otherwise, its tinted glass reveals nothing. My roommates told me this was a fancy dessert and wine type place that could impress for a Valentine's Day date.

When we walk inside, it reminds me of a fancy Starbucks with tables and no barista bar. They're playing indie acoustic music, the whole joint smells like coffee, and there are dark nooks everywhere for couples to get lost in.

After giving my name for the reservation, we're escorted to our table.

We sit down, perusing the menu, and my stomach drops. These desserts are so ... extra. Every recipe has some kind of elderflower or cayenne pepper or root vegetable infusion. What happened to a good piece of cheesecake, or a scoop of ice cream? Is this the rich people shit Jolie is into?

Across the table, Jolie smiles wearily at me.

"What's wrong?" I ask, alarm bells going off.

"Why did you pick this place?" she asks curiously.

I shrug. "I thought it would be romantic, and you know ... your kind of caliber of restaurant."

She blinks at me, then starts cracking up. "Come on, babe! Haven't we established that you could take me to Baskin Robbins and I'd be the happiest girl on the planet?"

I slap a hand to my forehead, because my attempt at romance was way too rose-colored. "I'm sorry, I thought this would be so adult and what you were used to on occasions like this and—"

Jolie lays a hand over mine, and her eyes are so full of love. "Just being with you on this day is the best date ever. And the roses you brought to pick me up just sealed the deal. I don't need an expensive meal, especially one where they put peppers in the brownies because who the hell wants that?"

"No one," I say adamantly. "Absolutely no one wants that. Or key lime froth with chickpea ice cream."

We both shiver as if it's the most disgusting thing we could ever eat, because it is.

She looks at me across from our tragically bad desserts and gives me one of those signature flirty smiles. "We could just blow this ridiculous popsicle stand and go do what we do best."

"And what's that?" I play with her fingers on the table.

Jolie leans in and lowers her voice. "Go have sex in a completely inappropriate spot."

My cock tingles just thinking about it. "Ah, our favorite pastime on our first official couple's holiday. I like how your brain works."

"I thought you might. I saw a secluded park not too far from the parking garage."

I throw down a twenty for their trouble, not sure what this fancy establishment charges for a brownie that induces coughing and copious amounts of water. Jolie takes my hand, and we scamper out of the restaurant, two lusted up addicts.

It's the perfect way to celebrate Valentine's Day; a tribute to how we fell in love, and a celebration of the spontaneity we'll never lose. It doesn't take science or logic to explain how we work, or why our connection will never be broken.

I get to be with the only girl I've ever loved, and that doesn't require my brain.

It's all heart.

EPILOGUE
JOLIE

Two Years Later

I tap my foot incessantly, waiting to get off the plane.

You know those people that are annoying and stand the minute the seatbelt sign comes off even though the plane is still taxiing? Yeah, that's me. Usually, I do it anyway, because what is this life if you can't jump up and be aggressive in it? But today, it's especially true.

I've been gone for a week, and somewhere in the arrivals pickup area, Mick is waiting for me.

I know to most couples, a week isn't anything, but we haven't gone this long without seeing each other since winter break two years ago. Since we became an official, exclusive pair, we've spent almost every day, including holidays and weekends, with each other.

The girl in front of me, who is standing in front of the exact place I need to step into to grab my bag in the overhead compartment, gives me a dirty look. I shrug and give her an apologetic nod. But can you blame me?

I'm horny and my hot doctor boyfriend is waiting in the airport for me.

Well, sort of a doctor. Mick is in his second year of medical school and kicking ass, having been accepted with top honors into the Salem Walsh Medical School. He's studying to be a neurologist, just like Dr. Richards, and hasn't stopped his work on his mentor's trial. I try to keep pace with what he's talking about when he comes home at the end of the day, but most of the scientific stuff goes over my head. All I know is that he's changing the world, and I'm so proud and turned on by it. Seriously, it's freaking hot to have a future doctor as a boyfriend.

They let us deplane, and it feels like the slowest walk ever to get out of the tunnel and start passing people through the airport. I'm like one of those pedestrians in New York, practically side swiping people to get to my destination.

My plane arrived in North Carolina from California, where I've been at the brand's headquarters for our annual sales summit. I don't think I could be any more inspired or fired up by the presentations and seminars I sat in on this entire week.

I'm working as a sales rep for one of my favorite makeup brands. I cover the North Carolina territories, lugging my kits and bags to Sephoras, Ultas, and department stores across the state. I meet with top officials for those brands in this area to sell them on our latest product, checkup about supplies, or promote our latest monthly deals.

When I went into the interview gushing about their best products and basically fangirling over all the things I knew about the brand, I think they knew they had to hire me. If nothing else, then the fact that no one else would sell their brand as desperately and obnoxiously as I would.

And the job is perfect for me. It combines my bubbly, chatty personality with my competitive nature. I make commission and bonuses, or get prize packs, for hitting certain numbers every quarter. It's a healthy level of fear that keeps me on my toes, and I have a feeling I'd be bored in any other job. Plus, I literally get to play with makeup all day, and who wouldn't love that?

But I'm glad to be home. I'm glad to have a few days off with my man to just reconnect and wear our mattress out. We moved into an apartment near campus a year ago, after I graduated as a senior from Salem Walsh and Mick was finishing up his first year of medical school. It's nothing fancy, but it's ours, and we've worked together to make it a home. I even conceded to putting some of Mick's weird science pun posters in a part of the living room—although guests would never be able to see them if they didn't know they were there.

Most weekends, if he is off his clinical rotation, we make the two-hour drive to see Mick's Mom. I haven't kept in touch with my own much, and have refused their financial or job-related help every time they offer, so it's nice to be a small part of an actual family.

Unfortunately, Mick's father passed shortly after his son's undergraduate graduation. In the months leading up to his death, his father regressed at a rapid pace, and no amount of science or otherwise could keep him with us. Mick spent every day for two months at his bedside, and deferred some of his summer medical studies to simply be with his father in his final moments. It was both crushing and humbling to watch.

After living with ALS for six years, his father outlived more than eighty percent of patients diagnosed in terms of life expectancy. I know that doesn't sound like a victory, but Mick uses his father's case in his research daily, both to emotionally fuel him and to gather evidence and theories about how to extend the life expectancy of those living with this terrible disease.

He had a rough time after his dad's death, understandably. It took a good year for the grief process to work itself out, and there are still days where I wake up and just know it will be a hellish one for the man I love. I know it's not the most comforting, and I rarely speak these words out loud, but Mick is truly lucky he got the years he did with his father, and to have the father he was blessed with. So many people don't get one day with a man like that, and I know I'm a changed person just for having known him a short time.

I'm practically sprinting through the airport at this point, and as I round the barrier, I see a giant mess of balloons, and practically squeal. Mick has learned over the years that it doesn't take fancy dinners or expensive presents to make me happy. Trust me, I love those, but I've known them my whole life, and those things never brought caring, love or a deeper connection to the person giving them. No, he's learned that I love a corny, ridiculous romantic gesture. Like rose petals on the floor to our bedroom or spinning me around to dance in the middle of the grocery aisle. And he never disappoints.

I run to him, not giving a flying fuck who is watching us giddy twenty-somethings greet each other. He catches me at full speed, my legs wrapping around his waist, as he drops the sign he was holding. Yep, my boyfriend picked me up from the airport with balloons and homemade poster board that reads "Welcome Home, Beautiful."

It's such a contrast from my nerdy, no-nonsense man, but he does it for me because he knows I love it. That's what makes it even more special.

"I missed you." He presses a kiss to my temple as I burrow into the crook of his neck.

"I missed you." I breathe in his minty scent.

"People are starting to stare." He chuckles, lowering me to the ground.

I shrug. "Let them, they're just jealous. You're so sweet, I love the balloons."

"People looked at me like I was a circus clown for the last half an hour. It was worth it though." Mick bends to kiss me.

His mouth is warm and I've ached for it for seven days straight. I could get much friskier in this airport and have to pull back before I don't have the willpower to stop myself.

"I want to do things with you. In that lab coat." I wiggle my eyebrows.

Mick rolls his eyes, but chuckles. "You and that lab coat. I think you like that thing more than me these days."

"It really adds something extra." I wink, already tingling south of my waistline.

"Let's get out of here. I have a surprise for you in the car." He smirks at me.

I grab his hand, lacing my fingers through it. "It doesn't happen to be a milkshake, because that would just make this whole thing better."

I may or may not have texted him that I wanted a chocolate milkshake from my favorite ice cream place, so it isn't that much of a surprise.

"I love you." He laughs as we make our way to his car.

"I love you." I snuggle into his shoulder.

The word I don't add to the end of it is *more*, because I know he'll only start debating with me. But I do. I love him just a teeny bit more, because I'm the emotional one and because he's showed me a life where loving someone means being there for them in their most wonderful times and their most ugly times.

Who knew that my secret fling from summer camp would end up being my forever? I had no idea back then how much skinny dipping in a fountain would change my life.

But I'm damn glad it did.

Do you want your **FREE** Carrie Aarons eBook?

All you have to do is **<u>sign up for my newsletter</u>**, and you'll immediately receive your free book!

ALSO BY CARRIE AARONS

All of my books are currently enrolled in Kindle Unlimited.

The Lion Heart

The Mighty Anchor

The Nash Brothers Series:

Fleeting

Forgiven

Flutter

Falter

The Flipped Series:

Blind Landing

Grasping Air

The Captive Heart Duet:

Lost

Found

The Over the Fence Series:

Pitching to Win

Hitting to Win

Catching to Win

ABOUT THE AUTHOR

Author of romance novels such as The Tenth Girl and Privileged, Carrie Aarons writes books that are just as swoon-worthy as they are sarcastic. A former journalist, she prefers the love stories of her imagination, and the athleisure dress code, much better.

When she isn't writing, Carrie is busy binging reality TV, having a love/hate relationship with cardio, and trying not to burn dinner. She's a Jersey girl living in Texas with her husband, daughter, son and Great Dane/Lab rescue.

Please join her readers group, Carrie's Charmers, to get the latest on new books, as well as talk about reality TV, wine and home decor.

You can also find Carrie at these places:
Website
Facebook
Instagram
Twitter
Amazon
Goodreads

CPSIA information can be obtained
at www.ICGtesting.com
Printed in the USA
LVHW041734170920
666361LV00005B/852